It was ten thirty when Jimmy ... ant. He entered with his own latchk... ut-ton which lighted the stairwa... ng above, and, ascending, went ... r. Compton's office, turned the k... d the door, to find that the interio...

"Strange," he thought, "that after sending for me the fellow didn't wait." As these thoughts passed through his mind he fumbled on the wall for the switch, and, finding it, flooded the office with light.

As he turned again toward the room he voiced a sudden exclamation of horror, for on the floor beside his desk lay the body of Mason Compton!

A SPECIAL ANNOUNCEMENT TO ALL ERB ENTHUSIASTS

Because of the widespread, continuing interest in the books of Edgar Rice Burroughs, we are listing below the names and addresses of various ERB fan club magazines. Additional information may be obtained from the editors of the magazines themselves.

—THE EDITORS

ERB-DOM MAGAZINE
Route 2, Box 119
Clinton, LA 70722

THE BURROUGHS BIBLIOPHILES
6657 Locust Street
Kansas City, Missouri 64131

ERBANIA MAGAZINE
8001 Fernview Lane
Tampa, Florida 33615

EDGAR RICE BURROUGHS

THE EFFICIENCY EXPERT

A DIVISION OF CHARTER COMMUNICATIONS INC.
A GROSSET & DUNLAP COMPANY

THE EFFICIENCY EXPERT

Copyright © 1966 by Edgar Rice Burroughs, Inc.
Originally published by House of Greystoke
All Rights Reserved

Published by arrangement with Edgar Rice Burroughs, Inc.

Charter Books
A Division of Charter Communications Inc.
A Grosset & Dunlap Company
360 Park Avenue South
New York, New York 10010

2 4 6 8 0 9 7 5 3 1
Manufactured in the United States of America

Contents

THE EFFICIENCY EXPERT

Part One

1

JIMMY TORRANCE, JR.

THE gymnasium was packed as Jimmy Torrance stepped into the ring for the final event of the evening that was to decide the boxing championship of the university. Drawing to a close were the nearly four years of his college career—profitable years, Jimmy considered them, and certainly successful up to this point. In the beginning of his senior year he had captained the varsity eleven, and in the coming spring he would again sally forth upon the diamond as the star initial sacker of collegedom.

His football triumphs were in the past, his continued baseball successes a foregone conclusion—if he won to-night his cup of happiness, and an unassailably dominant position among his fellows, would be assured, leaving nothing more, in so far as Jimmy reasoned, to be desired from four years attendance at one of America's oldest and most famous universities.

The youth who would dispute the right to championship honors with Jimmy was a dark horse to the extent that he was a freshman, and, therefore, practically unknown. He had worked hard, however, and given a good account of himself in his preparations for the battle, and there were rumors, as there always are about every campus, of marvelous exploits prior to his college days. It was even darkly hinted that he was a professional pugilist. As a matter of fact, he was the best exponent of the manly art of self-defense that Jimmy Torrance had ever faced, and in addition thereto he outweighed the senior and outreached him.

The boxing contest, as the faculty members of the athletic committee preferred to call it, was, from the tap of the gong, as pretty a two-fisted scrap as ever any aggregation of low-browed fight-fans witnessed. The details of this gory encounter, while interesting, have no particular bearing upon the development of this tale. What interests us is the outcome, which occurred in the middle of a very bloody fourth round, in which Jimmy Torrance scored a clean knock-out.

It was a battered but happy Jimmy who sat in his room the following Monday afternoon, striving to concentrate his mind upon a college text-book which should, by all the laws of fiction, have been "well thumbed," but in reality possessed unruffled freshness which belied its real age.

"I wish," mused Jimmy, "that I could have got to the bird who invented mathematics before he inflicted all this unnecessary anguish upon an already unhappy world. In about three rounds I could have saved thousands from the sorrow which I feel every time I open this blooming book."

He was still deeply engrossed in the futile attempt of accomplishing in an hour that for which the college curriculum set aside several months when there came sounds of approaching footsteps rapidly ascending the stairway. His door was unceremoniously thrown open, and there appeared one of those strange apparitions which is the envy and despair of the small-town youth—a naturally good-looking young fellow, the sartorial arts of whose tailor had elevated his waist-line to his armpits, dragged down his shoulders, and caved in his front until he had the appearance of being badly dished from chin to knees. His trousers appeared to have been made for a man with legs six inches longer than his, while his hat was evidently several sizes too large, since it would have entirely extinguished his face had it not been supported by his ears.

"Hello, Kid!" cried Jimmy. "What's new?"

"Whiskers wants you," replied the other. "Faculty meeting. They just got through with me."

"Hell!" muttered Jimmy feelingly. "I don't know what Whiskers wants with me, but he never wants to see anybody about anything pleasant."

"I am here," agreed the other, "to announce to the universe that you are right, Jimmy. He didn't have anything pleasant to say to me. In fact, he insinuated that dear old alma mater might be able to wiggle along without me if I didn't abjure my criminal life. Made some nasty comparison between my academic achievements and fox-trotting. I wonder, Jimmy, how they get that way?"

"That's why they are profs," explained Jimmy. "There are two kinds of people in the world—human beings and profs. When does he want me?"

"Now."

Jimmy arose and put on his hat and coat. "Good-by, Kid," he said. "Pray for me, and leave me one cigarette to smoke when I get back," and, grinning, he left the room.

James Torrance, Jr., was not greatly abashed as he faced the dour tribunal of the faculty. The younger members, among whom were several he knew to be mighty good fellows at heart, sat at the lower end of the long table, and with owlish gravity attempted to emulate the appearance and manners of their seniors. At the head of the table sat Whiskers, as the dignified and venerable president of the university was popularly named. It was generally believed and solemnly sworn to throughout the large corps of undergraduates that within the knowledge of any living man Whiskers had never been known to smile, and to-day he was running true to form.

"Mr. Torrance," he said, sighing, "it has been my painful duty on more than one occasion to call your attention to the uniformly low average of your academic standing. At the earnest solicitation of the faculty members of the athletic committee, I have been influenced, against my better judgment, to temporize with an utterly insufferable condition.

"You are rapidly approaching the close of your senior year, and in the light of the records which I have before me I am constrained to believe that it will be utterly impossible for you to graduate, unless from now to the end of the semester you devote yourself exclusively to your academic work. If you cannot assure me that you will do this, I believe it would be to the best interests of the university for you to resign now, rather than to fail of graduation. And in this decision I am fully seconded by the faculty members of the athletic committee, who realize the harmful effect upon university athletics in the future were so prominent an athlete as you to fail at graduation."

If they had sentenced Jimmy to be shot at sunrise the blow could scarcely have been more stunning than that which followed the realization that he was not to be permitted to round out his fourth successful season at first base. But if Jimmy was momentarily stunned he gave no outward indication of the fact, and in the brief interval of silence following the president's ultimatum his alert mind functioned with the rapidity which it had often shown upon the gridiron, the diamond, and the squared circle.

Just for a moment the thought of being deprived of the pleasure and excitement of the coming baseball season filled his mind to the exclusion of every other consideration, but presently a less selfish impulse projected upon the screen of recollection the figure of the father he idolized. The boy realized the disappointment that this man would feel should his four years of college end thus disastrously and without the coveted diploma.

And then it was that he raised his eyes to those of the president.

"I hope, sir," he said, "that you will give me one more chance—that you will let me go on as I have in the past as far as baseball is concerned, with the understanding that if at the end of each month between now and commencement I do not show satisfactory improvement I shall not be permitted to play on the team. But please don't make that restriction binding yet. If I lay off the track work I believe I can make up enough so that baseball will not interfere with my graduation."

And so Whiskers, who was much more human that the student body gave him credit for being, and was, in the bargain, a good judge of boys, gave Jimmy another chance on his own terms, and the university's heavyweight champion returned to his room filled with determination to make good at the eleventh hour.

Possibly one of the greatest obstacles which lay in Jimmy's path toward academic honors was the fact that he possessed those qualities of character which attracted others to him, with the result that there was seldom an hour during the day that he had his room to himself. On his return from the faculty meeting he found a half-dozen of his classmates there, awaiting his return.

"Well?" they inquired as he entered.

"It's worse than that," said Jimmy, as he unfolded the harrowing details of what had transpired at his meeting with the faculty. "And now," he said, "if you birds love me, keep out of here from now until commencement. There isn't a guy on earth can concentrate on anything with a roomful of you mental ciphers sitting around and yapping about girls and other non-essential creations."

"Non-essential!" gasped one of his visitors, letting his eyes wander over the walls of Jimmy's study, whereon were nailed, pinned or hung countless framed and unframed pictures of non-essential creations.

"All right, Jimmy," said another. "We are with you, horse, foot and artillery. When you want us, give us the high-sign and we will come. Otherwise we will leave you to your beloved books. It is too bad, though, as the bar-boy was just explaining how the great drought might be circumvented by means of carrots, potato peelings, dish-water, and a raisin."

"Go on," said Jimmy; "I am not interested," and the boys left him to his "beloved" books.

Jimmy Torrance worked hard, and by dint of long hours and hard-working tutors he finished his college course and won his diploma. Nor did he have to forego the crowning honors of his last baseball season, although, like Ulysses S. Grant, he would have graduated at the head of his class had the list been turned upside down.

2

JIMMY WILL ACCEPT A POSITION.

FOLLOWING his graduation he went to New York to visit with one of his classmates for a short time before returning home. He was a very self-satisfied Jimmy, nor who can wonder, since almost from his matriculation there had been constantly dinned into his ears the plaudits of his fellow students. Jimmy Torrance had been the one big, outstanding figure of each succeeding class from his freshman to his senior year, and as junior and senior he had been the acknowledged leader of the student body and as popular a man as the university had ever known.

To his fellows, as well as to himself, he had been a great success—*the* success of the university—and he and they saw in the future only continued success in whatever vocation he decided to honor with his presence. It was in a mental attitude that had become almost habitual with him, and which was superinduced by these influences, that Jimmy approached the new life that was opening before him. For a while he would play, but in the fall it was his firm intention to settle down to some serious occupation, and it was in this attitude that he opened a letter from his father—the first that he had received since his graduation.

The letter was written on the letterhead of the Beatrice Corn Mills, Incorporated, Beatrice, Nebraska, and in the upper left-hand corner, in small type, appeared "James Torrance, Sr., President and General Manager," and this is what he read:

DEAR JIM:

You have graduated—I didn't think you would —with honors in football, baseball, prize-fighting, and five thousand dollars in debt. How you got your diploma is beyond me—in my day you would have got the sack. Well, son, I am not surprised nor disappointed—it is what I expected. I know you are clean, though, and that some day you will awaken to the sterner side of life and an appreciation of your responsibilities.

To be an entirely orthodox father I should raise merry hell about your debts and utter inutility, at the same time disinheriting you, but instead I am going to urge you to come home and run in debt here where the cost of living is not so high as in the East—meanwhile praying that your awakening may come while I am on earth to rejoice.

Your affectionate
FATHER

Am enclosing check to cover your debts and present needs.

For a long time the boy sat looking at the letter before him. He reread it once, twice, three times, and with each reading the film of unconscious egotism that had blinded him to his own shortcomings gradually became less opaque, until finally he saw himself as his father must see him. He had come to college for the purpose of fitting himself to succeed in some particular way in the stern battle of life which must follow his graduation; for, though his father had ample means to support him in indolence, Jimmy had never even momentarily considered such an eventuality.

In weighing his assets now he discovered that he had probably as excellent a conception of gridiron strategy and tactics as any man in America; that as a boxer he occupied a position in the forefront of amateur ranks; and he was quite positive that outside of the major leagues there was not a better first baseman.

But in the last few minutes there had dawned upon him the realization that none of these accomplishments was greatly in demand in the business world. Jimmy spent a very blue and unhappy hour, and then slowly his natural optimism reasserted itself, and with it came the realization of his youth and strength and inherent ability which, without egotism, he might claim.

"And then, too," he mused, "I have my diploma, I am a college graduate, and that must mean something. If dad had only reproached me or threatened some condign punishment I don't believe I should feel half as badly as I do. But every line of that letter breathes disappointment in me; and yet, God bless him, he tells me to come home and spend his money there. Not on your life! If he won't disinherit me, I am going to disinherit myself. I am going to make him proud of me. He's the best dad a fellow ever had, and I am going to show him that I appreciate him."

And so he sat down and wrote his father this reply:

DEAR DAD:

I have your letter and check. You may not believe it, but the former is worth more to me than the latter. Not, however, that I spurn the check, which it was just like you to send without a lot of grumbling and reproaches, even if I do deserve them.

Your letter has shown me what a rotten mess I have made of myself. I'm not going to hand you a lot of mush, dad, but I want to try to do something that will give you reason to at least have hopes of rejoicing before I come home again. If I fail I'll come home anyway, and then neither one of us will have any doubt but what you will have to support me for the rest of my life. However, I don't intend to fail, and one of these days I will bob up all serene as president of a bank or a glue factory. In the mean time I'll keep you posted as to my whereabouts, but don't send me another cent until I ask for it; and when I do you will know that I have failed.

Tell mother that I will write her in a day or two, probably from Chicago, as I have always had an idea that that was one burg where I could make good.

With lots of love to you all,

Your affectionate

SON

It was a hot July day that James Torrance, Jr.,

alighted from the Twentieth Century Limited at the LaSalle Street Station, and, entering a cab, directed that he be driven to a small hotel; "for," he soliloquized, "I might as well start economizing at once, as it might be several days before I land a job such as I want," in voicing which sentiments he spoke with the tongues of the prophets.

Jimmy had many friends in Chicago with whom, upon the occasion of numerous previous visits to the Western metropolis, he had spent many hilarious and expensive hours, but now he had come upon the serious business of life, and there moved within him a strong determination to win financial success without recourse to the influence of rich and powerful acquaintances.

Since the first crushing blow that his father's letter had dealt his egotism, Jimmy's self-esteem had been gradually returning, though along new and more practical lines. His self-assurance was formed in a similar mold to those of all his other salient characteristics, and these conformed to his physical proportions, for physically, mentally and morally Jimmy Torrance was big; not that he was noticeably taller than other men or his features more than ordinarily attractive, but there was something so well balanced and harmonious in all the proportions of his frame and features as to almost invariably compel a second glance from even a casual observer, especially if the casual observer happened to be in the non-essential creation class.

And so Jimmy, having had plenty of opportunity to commune with himself during the journey from New York, was confident that there were many opportunities awaiting him in Chicago. He remembered distinctly of having read somewhere that the growing need of business concerns was competent executive material—that there were fewer big men than there were big jobs—and that if such was the case all that remained to be done was to connect himself with the particular big job that suited him.

In the lobby of the hotel he bought several of the daily papers, and after reaching his room he started perusing the "Help Wanted" columns. Immediately he was impressed and elated by the discovery that there were plenty of jobs, and that a satisfactory percentage of them appeared to be big jobs. There were so many, however, that appealed to him as excellent possibilities that he saw it would be impossible to apply for each and every one; and then it occurred to him that he might occupy a more strategic position in the negotiations preceding his acceptance of a position if his future employer came to him first, rather than should he be the one to apply for the position.

And so he decided the wisest plan would be to insert an ad in the "Situations Wanted" column, and then from the replies select those which most appealed to him; in other words, he would choose from the cream of those who desired the services of such a man as himself rather than risk the chance of obtaining a less profitable position through undue haste in seizing upon the first opening advertised.

Having reached this decision, and following his habitual custom, he permitted no grass to grow beneath his feet. Writing out an ad, he reviewed it carefully, compared it with others that he saw upon the printed page, made a few changes, rewrote it, and then descended to the lobby, where he called a cab and was driven to the office of one of the great metropolitan morning newspapers.

Jimmy felt very important as he passed through the massive doorway into the great general offices of the newspaper. Of course, he didn't exactly expect that he would be ushered into the presence of the president or business manager, or that even the advertising manager would necessarily have to pass upon his copy, but there was within him a certain sensation that at that instant something was transpiring that in later years would be a matter of great moment, and he was really very sorry for the publishers of the newspaper that they did not know who it was who was inserting an ad in their Situations Wanted column.

He could not help but watch the face of the young man who received his ad and counted the words, as he was sure that the clerk's facial expression would betray his excitement. It was a great moment for Jimmy Torrance. He realized that it was probably the greatest moment of his life—that here Jimmy Torrance ceased to be, and James Torrance, Jr., Esq., began his career. But though he carefully watched the face of the clerk, he was finally forced to admit that the young man possessed wonderful control over his facial expression.

"That bird has a regular poker-face," mused Jimmy; "never batted an eye," and paying for his ad he pocketed the change and walked out.

"Let's see," he figured; "it will be in tomorrow morning's edition. The tired business man will read it either at breakfast or after he reaches his office. I understand that there are three million people here in Chicago. Out of that three million it is safe to assume that one million will read my advertisement, and of that one million there must be at least one thousand who have responsible positions which are, at present, inadequately filled.

"Of course, the truth of the matter is that there are probably tens of thousands of such positions, but to be conservative I will assume that there are only one thousand, and reducing it still further to almost an absurdity, I will figure that only ten per cent of those reply to my advertisement. In other words, at the lowest possible estimate I should have one hundred replies on the first day. I knew it was foolish to run it for three days, but the fellow insisted that that was the proper way to do, as I got a lower rate.

"By taking it for three days, however, it doesn't seem right to make so many busy men waste their time answering the ad when I shall doubtless find a satisfactory position the first day."

3

THE LIZARD

THAT night Jimmy attended a show, and treated himself to a lonely dinner afterward. He should have liked very much to have looked up some of his friends. A telephone call would have brought invitations to dinner and a pleasant evening with convivial companions, but he had mapped his course and he was determined to stick to it to the end.

"There will be plenty of time," he thought, "for amusement after I have gotten a good grasp of my new duties." Jimmy elected to walk from the theater to his hotel, and as he was turning the corner from Randolph into La Salle a young man jostled him. An instant later the stranger was upon his knees, his wrist doubled suddenly backward and very close to the breaking-point.

"Wot t' hell yuh doin'?" he screamed.

"Pardon me," replied Jimmy; "you got your hand in the wrong pocket. I suppose you meant to put it in your own, but you didn't."

"Aw, g'wan; lemme go," pleaded the stranger. "I didn't get nuthin'—you ain't got the goods on me."

Now, such a tableau as Jimmy and his new acquaintance formed cannot be staged at the corner of Randolph and La Salle beneath an arc light, even at midnight, without attracting attention. And so it was that before Jimmy realized it a dozen curious pedestrians were approaching them from different directions, and a burly blue-coated figure was shouldering his way forward.

Jimmy had permitted his captive to rise, but he still held tightly to his wrist as the officer confronted them. He took one look at Jimmy's companion, and then grabbed him roughly by the arm. "So, it's you again, is it?" he growled.

"I ain't done nuthin'," muttered the man.

The officer looked inquiringly at Jimmy.

"What's all the excitement about?" asked the latter. "My friend and I have done nothing."

"Your fri'nd and you?" replied the policeman. "He ain't no fri'nd o' yours, or yez wouldn't be sayin' so."

"Well, I'll admit," replied Jimmy, "that possibly I haven't known him long enough to presume to claim any close friendship, but there's no telling what time may develop."

"You don't want him pinched?" asked the policeman.

"Of course not," replied Jimmy. "Why should he be pinched?"

The officer turned roughly upon the stranger, shook him viciously a few times, and then gave him a mighty shove which all but sent him sprawling into the gutter.

"G'wan wid yez," he yelled after him, "and if I see ye on this beat again I'll run yez in. An' you"—he turned upon Jimmy—"ye'd betther be on your way and not be afther makin' up with ivery dip ye meet."

"Thanks," said Jimmy. "Have a cigar."

After the officer had helped himself and condescended to relax his stern features into the semblance of a smile the young man bid him good night and resumed his way toward the hotel.

"Pretty early to go to bed," he thought as he reached for his watch to note the time, running his fingers into an empty pocket. Gingerly he felt in another pocket, where he knew his watch couldn't possibly be, nor was. Carefully Jimmy examined each pocket of his coat and trousers, a slow and broad grin illumining his face.

"What do you know about that?" he mused. "And I thought I was a wise guy."

A few minutes after Jimmy reached his room the office called him on the telephone to tell him that a man had called to see him.

"Send him up," said Jimmy, wondering who it might be, since he was sure that no one knew of his presence in the city. He tried to connect the call in some way with his advertisement, but inasmuch as that had been inserted blind he felt that there could be no possible connection between that and his caller.

A few minutes later there was a knock on his door, and in response to his summons to enter the door opened, and there stood before him the young man of his recent encounter upon the street. The latter entered softly, closing the door behind him. His feet made no sound upon the carpet, and no sound came from the door as he closed it, nor any slightest click from the latch. His utter silence and the stealth of his movements were so pronounced as to attract immediate attention. He did not speak until he had reached the center of the room and halted on the opposite side of the table at which Jimmy was standing; and then a very slow smile moved his lips, though the expression of his eyes remained unchanged.

"Miss anything?" he asked.

"Yes," said Jimmy.

"Here it is," said the visitor, laying the other's watch upon the table.

"Why this spasm of virtue?" asked Jimmy.

"Oh, I don't know," replied the other. "I guess it's because you're a white guy. O'Donnell has been trying to get something on me for the last year. He's got it in for me—I wouldn't cough every time the big stiff seen me."

"Sit down," said Jimmy.

"Naw," said the other; "I gotta be goin'."

"Come," insisted the host; "sit down for a few minutes at least. I was just wishing that I had some one to talk to."

The other sank noiselessly into a chair. "All right, bo," he said.

Jimmy proffered him his cigar-case.

"No, thanks," declined the visitor. "I'd rather have a coffin-nail," which Jimmy forthwith furnished.

"I should think," said Jimmy, "that your particular line of endeavor would prove rather hazardous in a place where you are known by the police."

The other smiled and, as before, with his lips alone.

"Naw," he said; "this is the safest place to work. If ten per cent of the bulls know me I got that much on them, and then some, because any boob can spot any one o' de harness bunch, and I know nearly every fly on the department. They're the guys yuh gotta know, and usually I know something besides their names, too," and again his lips smiled.

"How much of your time do you have to put in at your occupation to make a living?" asked Jimmy.

"Sometimes I put in six or eight hours a day," replied the visitor. "De rush hours on de surface line are usually good for two or t'ree hours a day, but I been layin' off dat stuff lately and goin' in fer de t'ater crowd. Dere's more money and shorter hours."

"You confine yourself," asked Jimmy, "to—er—ah—pocket-picking solely?"

Again the lip smile. "I'll tell youse sumpin', bo, dat dey don't none o' dem big stiffs on de department know. De dip game is a stall. I learned it when I was a kid, an' dese yaps t'ink dat's all I know, and I keep dem t'inkin' it by pullin' stuff under der noses often enough to give 'em de hunch dat I'm still at de same ol' business." He leaned confidentially across the table. "If you ever want a box cracked, look up the Lizard."

"Meaning?" asked Jimmy.

"Me, bo; I'm the Lizard."

"Box cracked?" repeated Jimmy. "An ice-box or a hot box?"

His visitor grinned. "Safe," he explained.

"Oh," said Jimmy, "if I ever want any one to break into a safe, come to you, huh?"

"You get me," replied the other.

"All right," said Jimmy, laughing. "I'll call on you. That the only name you got, Mr. Lizard?"

"That's all—just the Lizard. Now I gotta be beatin' it."

"Goin' to crack a box?" asked Jimmy.

The other smiled his lip smile and turned toward the door.

"Wait a second," said Jimmy. "What would you have gotten on this watch of mine?"

"It would have stood me about twenty bucks."

Jimmy reached into his pocket and drew forth a roll of bills. "Here," he said, handing the other two tens.

"Naw," said the Lizard, shoving the proffered money away. "I'm no cheap skate."

"Come on—take it," said Jimmy. "I may want a box cracked some day."

"All right," said the Lizard, "if you put it that way, bo."

"I should think," said Jimmy, "that a man of your ability could earn a living by less precarious methods."

"You would think so," replied the Lizard. "I've tried two or three times to go straight. Wore out my shoes looking for a job. Never landed anything that paid me more than ten bucks per, and worked nine or ten hours a day, and half the time I couldn't get that."

"I suppose the police hounded you all the time, too," suggested Jimmy.

"Naw," said the Lizard; "dat's all bunk. De fellows that couldn't even float down a sewer straight pull dat. Once in a while dey get it in for some guy, but dey're glad enough to leave us alone if we leave dem alone. I worked four hours to-day, maybe six before I get through, and I'll stand a chance of makin' all the way from fifty dollars to five thousand. Suppose I was drivin' a milk-wagon, gettin' up at t'ree o'clock in the mornin' and workin' like hell—how much would I get out of dat? Expectin' every minute some one was goin' tuh fire me. Nuthin' doin'—dey can't nobody fire me now. I'm my own boss."

"Well," said Jimmy, "your logic sounds all right, but it all depends upon the viewpoint. But I'll tell you: you've offered me your services; I'll offer you mine. Whenever you want a job, look me up. I'm going to be general manager of a big concern here, and you'll find me in the next issue of the telephone directory." He handed the Lizard his card.

"T'anks," said the latter. "If you don't want a box cracked any sooner than I want a job, the chances are we will never meet again. So-long," and he was gone as noiselessly as he had come.

Jimmy breakfasted at nine the next morning, and as he waited for his bacon and eggs he searched the Situations Wanted columns of the morning paper until his eye finally alighted upon that for which he sought—the ad that was to infuse into the business life of the great city a new and potent force. Before his breakfast was served Jimmy had read the few lines over a dozen times, and with each succeeding reading he was more and more pleased with the result of his advertising ability as it appeared in print:

> WANTED—By College Graduate—Position as General Manager of Large Business where ability, energy and experience will be appreciated. Address 263-S, Tribune Office.

He had decided to wait until after lunch before calling at the newspaper office for replies to his advertisement, but during breakfast it occurred to him there probably would be several alert prospective employers who would despatch their replies by special messengers, and realizing that promptness was one of the cardinal virtues in the business world, Jimmy reasoned that it would make a favorable impression were he to present himself as soon as possible after the receipt of replies.

By a simple system of reasoning he deduced that ten o'clock would be none too early to expect some returns from his ad, and therefore at ten promptly he presented himself at the Want Ad Department in the *Tribune* office.

Comparing the number of the receipt which Jimmy handed him with the numbers upon a file of little pigeonholes, the clerk presently turned back toward the counter with a handful of letters.

"Whew!" thought Jimmy. "I never would have guessed that I would receive a bunch like that so early in the morning." But then, as he saw the clerk running through them one by one, he realized that they were not all for him, and as the young man ran through them Jimmy's spirits dropped a notch with each letter that was passed over without being thrown out to him, until when the last letter had passed beneath the scrutiny of the clerk, and the advertiser realized that he had received no replies, he was quite sure that there was some error.

"Nothing," said the clerk, shaking his head negatively.

"Are you sure you looked in the right compartment?" asked Jimmy.

"Sure," replied the clerk. "There is nothing for you."

Jimmy pocketed his slip and walked from the office. "This town is slower than I thought it was," he mused. "I guess they do need some live wires here to manage their business."

At noon he returned, only to be again disappointed, and then at two o'clock, and when he came in at four the same clerk looked up wearily and shook his head.

"Nothing for you," he said. "I distributed all the stuff myself since you were in last."

As Jimmy stood there almost dazed by surprise that during an entire day his ad had appeared in Chicago's largest newspaper, and he had not received one reply, a man approached the counter, passed a slip similar to Jimmy's to the clerk, and received fully a hundred letters in return. Jimmy was positive now that something was wrong.

"Are you sure," he asked the clerk, "that my replies haven't been sidetracked somewhere? I have seen people taking letters away from here all day, and that bird there just walked off with a fistful."

The clerk grinned. "What you advertising for?" he asked.

"A position," replied Jimmy.

"That's the answer," explained the clerk. "That fellow there was advertising for help."

4

JIMMY HUNTS A JOB

ONCE again Jimmy walked out onto Madison Street, and, turning to his right, dropped into a continuous vaudeville show in an attempt to coax his spirits back to somewhere near their normal high-water mark. Upon the next day he again haunted the newspaper office without reward, and again upon the third day with similar results. To say that Jimmy was dumfounded would be but a futile description of his mental state. It was simply beyond him to conceive that in one of the largest cities in the world, the center of a thriving district of fifty million souls, there was no business man with sufficient acumen to realize how badly he needed James Torrance, Jr., to conduct his business for him successfully.

With the close of the fourth day, and no reply, Jimmy was thoroughly exasperated. The kindly clerk, who by this time had taken a personal interest in this steadiest of customers, suggested that Jimmy try applying for positions advertised in the Help Wanted column, and this he decided to do.

There were only two concerns advertising for general managers in the issue which Jimmy scanned; one ad called for an experienced executive to assume the general management of an old established sash, door and blind factory; the other insisted upon a man with mail-order experience to take charge of the mail-order department of a large department store.

Neither of these were precisely what Jimmy had hoped for, his preference really being for the general management of an automobile manufactory or possibly something in the airplane line. Sash, door and blind sounded extremely prosaic and uninteresting to Mr. Torrance. The mail-order proposition, while possibly more interesting, struck him as being too trifling and unimportant.

"However," he thought, "it will do no harm to have a talk with these people, and possibly I might even consider giving one of them a trial."

And so, calling a taxi, he drove out onto the west side where, in a dingy and squalid neighborhood, the taxi stopped in front of a grimy unpainted three-story brick building, from which a great deal of noise and dust were issuing. Jimmy found the office on the second floor, after ascending a narrow, dark, and dirty stairway. Jimmy's experience of manufacturing plants was extremely limited, but he needed no experience as he entered the room to see that he was in a busy office of a busy plant. Everything about the office was plain and rather dingy but there were a great many clerks and typists and considerable bustling about.

After stating his business to a young lady who

sat behind a switchboard, upon the front of which was the word "Information," and waiting while she communicated with an inner office over the telephone, he was directed in the direction of a glass partition at the opposite end of the room—a partition in which there were doors at intervals, and upon each door a name.

He had been told that Mr. Brown would see him, and rapping upon the door bearing that name he was bid to enter, and a moment later found himself in the presence of a middle-aged man whose every gesture and movement was charged with suppressed nerve energy.

As Jimmy entered the man was reading a letter. He finished it quickly, slapped it into a tray, and wheeled in his chair toward his caller.

"Well?" he snapped, as Jimmy approached him.

"I came in reply to your advertisement for a general manager," announced Jimmy confidently.

The man sized him up quickly from head to foot. His eyes narrowed and his brows contracted.

"What experience you had? Who you been with, and how many years?" He snapped the questions at Jimmy with the rapidity of machine-gun fire.

"I have the necessary ability," replied Jimmy, "to manage your business."

"How many years have you had in the sash, door and blind business?" snapped Mr. Brown.

"I have never had any experience in the sash, door and blind business," replied Jimmy. "I didn't come here to make sash, doors and blinds. I came here to manage your business."

Mr. Brown half rose from his chair. His eyes

opened a little wider than normal. "What the—" he started; and then, "Well, of all the—" Once again he found it impossible to go on. "You came here to manage a sash, door and blind factory, and don't know anything about the business! Well, of all—"

"I assumed," said Jimmy, "that what you wanted in a general manager was executive ability, and that's what I have."

"What you have," replied Mr. Brown, "is a hell of a crust. Now, run along, young fellow. I am a very busy man—and don't forget to close the door after you as you go out."

Jimmy did not forget to close the door. As he walked the length of the interminable room between rows of desks, before which were seated young men and young women, all of whom Jimmy thought were staring at him, he could feel the deep crimson burning upward from his collar to the roots of his hair.

Never before in his life had Jimmy's self-esteem received such a tremendous jolt. He was still blushing when he reached his cab, and as he drove back toward the Loop he could feel successive hot waves suffuse his countenance at each recollection of the humiliating scene through which he had just passed.

It was not until the next day that Jimmy had sufficiently reestablished his self-confidence to permit him to seek out the party who wished a mail-order manager, and while in this instance he met with very pleasant and gentlemanly treatment, his application was no less definitely turned down.

For a month Jimmy trailed one job after another. At the end of the first week he decided that the street-cars and sole leather were less expensive than taxicabs, as his funds were running perilously low; and he also lowered his aspirations successively from general managerships through departmental heads, assistants thereto, office managers, assistant office managers, and various other vocations, all with the same result; discovering meanwhile that experience, while possibly not essential as some of the ads stated, was usually the rock upon which his hopes were dashed.

He also learned something else which surprised him greatly: that rather than being an aid to his securing employment, his college education was a drawback, several men telling him bluntly that they had no vacancies for rah-rah boys.

At the end of the second week Jimmy had moved from his hotel to a still less expensive one, and a week later to a cheap boarding-house on the north side. At first he had written his father and his mother regularly, but now he found it difficult to write them at all. Toward the middle of the fourth week Jimmy had reached a point where he applied for a position as office-boy.

"I'll be damned if I'm going to quit," he said to himself, "if I have to turn street-sweeper. There must be some job here in the city that I am capable of filling, and I'm pretty sure that I can at least get a job as office-boy."

And so he presented himself to the office manager of a life-insurance company that had advertised such a vacancy. A very kindly gentleman interviewed him.

"What experience have you had?" he asked.

Jimmy looked at him aghast.

"Do I have to have experience to be an office-boy?" he asked.

"Well, of course," replied the gentleman, "it is not essential, but it is preferable. I already have applications from a dozen or more fellows, half of whom have had experience, and one in particular, whom I have about decided to employ, held a similar position with another life-insurance company."

Jimmy rose. "Good day," he said, and walked out.

That day he ate no lunch, but he had discovered a place where an abundance might be had for twenty-five cents if one knew how to order and ordered judiciously. And so to this place he repaired for his dinner. Perched upon a high stool, he filled at least a corner of the aching void within.

Sitting in his room that night he took account of his assets and his liabilities. His room rent was paid until Saturday night, and this was Thursday, and in his pocket were one dollar and sixty cents. Opening his trunk, he drew forth a sheet of paper and an envelope, and, clearing the top of the rickety little table which stood at the head of his bed, he sat down on the edge of the soiled counterpane and wrote a letter.

DEAR DAD:

I guess I'm through. I have tried and failed. It is hard to admit it, but I guess I'll have to. If you will send me the price I'll come home.

With love,

JIM.

Slowly he folded the letter and inserted it in the envelope, his face mirroring an utter dejection such as Jimmy Torrance had never before experienced in his life.

"Failure," he muttered, "unutterable failure."

Taking his hat, he walked down the creaking stairway, with its threadbare carpet, and out onto the street to post his letter.

5

JIMMY LANDS ONE

MISS ELIZABETH COMPTON sat in the dimly lighted library upon a deep-cushioned, tapestried sofa. She was not alone, yet although there were many comfortable chairs in the large room, and the sofa was an exceptionally long one, she and her companion occupied but little more space than would have comfortably accommodated a single individual.

"Stop it, Harold," she admonished. "I utterly loathe being mauled."

"But I can't help it, dear. It seems so absolutely wonderful! I can't believe it—that you are really mine."

"But I'm not—yet!" exclaimed the girl. "There are a lot of formalities and bridesmaids and ministers and things that have got to be taken into consideration before I am yours. And anyway there is no necessity for mussing me up so. You might as well know now as later that I utterly loathe this cave-man stuff. And really, Harold, there is nothing about your appearance that suggests a caveman, which is probably one reason that I like you."

"Like me?" exclaimed the young man. "I thought you loved me."

"I have to like you in order to love you, don't I?" she parried. "And one certainly has to like the man she is going to marry."

"Well," grumbled Mr. Bince, "you might be more enthusiastic about it."

"I prefer," explained the girl, "to be loved decorously. I do not care to be pawed or clawed or crumpled. After we have been married for fifteen or twenty years and are really well acquainted—"

"Possibly you will permit me to kiss you," Bince finished for her.

"Don't be silly, Harold," she retorted. "You have kissed me so much now that my hair is all down, and my face must be a sight. Lips are what you are supposed to kiss with—you don't have to kiss with your hands."

"Possibly I was a little bit rough. I am sorry," apologized the young man. "But when a fellow has just been told by the sweetest girl in the world that she will marry him, it's enough to make him a little bit crazy."

"Not at all," rejoined Miss Compton. "We should never forget the stratum of society to which we belong, and what we owe to the maintenance of the position we hold. My father has always impressed upon me the fact that gentlemen or gentlewomen are always gentle-folk under any and all circumstances and conditions. I distinctly recall his remark about one of his friends, whom he greatly admired, to this effect: that he always got drunk like a gentleman. Therefore we should do everything as gentle-folk should do things, and when we make love we should make love like gentle-folk, and not like hod-carriers or cavemen."

"Yes," said the young man; "I'll try to remember."

It was a little after nine o'clock when Harold Bince arose to leave.

"I'll drive you home," volunteered the girl. "Just wait, and I'll have Barry bring the roadster around."

"I thought we should always do the things that gentle-folk should do," said Bince, grinning, after being seated safely in the car. They had turned out of the driveway into Lincoln Parkway.

"What do you mean?" asked Elizabeth.

"Is it perfectly proper for young ladies to drive around the streets of a big city alone after dark?"

"But I'm not alone," she said.

"You will be after you leave me at home."

"Oh, well, I'm different."

"And I'm glad that you are!" exclaimed Bince fervently. "I wouldn't love you if you were like the ordinary run."

Bince lived at one of the down-town clubs, and after depositing him there and parting with a decorous handclasp the girl turned her machine and headed north for home. At Erie Street came a sudden loud hissing of escaping air.

"Darn!" exclaimed Miss Elizabeth Compton as she drew in beside the curb and stopped. Although she knew perfectly well that one of the tires was punctured, she got out and walked around in front as though in search of the cause of the disturbance, and sure enough, there it was, flat as a pancake, the left front tire.

There was an extra wheel on the rear of the roadster, but it was heavy and cumbersome, and the girl knew from experience what a dirty job changing a wheel is. She had just about decided to drive home on the rim, when a young man crossed the walk from Erie Street and joined her in her doleful appraisement of the punctured casing.

"Can I help you any?" he asked.

She looked up at him. "Thank you," she replied, "but I think I'll drive home on it as it is. They can change it there."

"It looks like a new casing," he said. "It would be too bad to ruin it. If you have a spare I will be very glad to change it for you," and without waiting for her acquiescence he stripped off his coat, rolled up his shirt-sleeves, and dove under the seat for the jack.

Elizabeth Compton was about to protest, but there was something about the way in which the stranger went at the job that indicated that he would probably finish it if he wished to, in spite of any arguments she could advance to the contrary. As he worked she talked with him, discovering not only that he was a rather nice person to look at, but that he was equally nice to talk to.

She could not help but notice that his clothes were rather badly wrinkled and that his shoes were dusty and well worn; for when he kneeled in the street to operate the jack the sole of one shoe was revealed beneath the light of an adjacent arc, and she saw that it was badly worn. Evidently he was a poor young man.

She had observed these things almost unconsciously, and yet they made their impression upon her, so that when he had finished she recalled them, and was emboldened thereby to offer him a bill in payment for his services. He refused, as she had almost expected him to do, for while his clothes and his shoes suggested that he might accept a gratuity, his voice and his manner belied them.

During the operation of changing the wheel the young man had a good opportunity to appraise the face and figure of the girl, both of which he found entirely to his liking, and when finally she started off, after thanking him, he stood upon the curb watching the car until it disappeared from view.

Slowly he drew from his pocket an envelope which had been addressed and stamped for mailing, and very carefully tore it into small bits which he dropped into the gutter. He could not have told had any one asked him what prompted him to the act. A girl had come into his life for an instant, and had gone out again, doubtless forever, and yet in that instant Jimmy Torrance had taken a new grasp upon his self-esteem.

It might have been the girl, and again it might not have been. He could not tell. Possibly it was the simple little act of refusing the tip she had proffered him. It might have been any one of a dozen little different things, or an accumulation of them all, that had brought back a sudden flood of the old self-confidence and optimism.

"To-morrow," said Jimmy as he climbed into his bed, "I am going to land a job."

And he did. In the department store to the general managership of whose mail-order department he had aspired Jimmy secured a position in the hosiery department at ten dollars a week. The department buyer who had interviewed him asked him what experience he had had with ladies' hosiery.

"About four or five years," replied Jimmy.

"For whom did you work?"

"I was in business for myself," replied the applicant, "both in the West and in the East. I got my first experience in a small town in Nebraska, but I carried on a larger business in the East later."

So they gave Jimmy a trial in a new section of the hosiery department, wherein he was the only male clerk. The buyer had discovered that there was a sufficient proportion of male customers, many of whom displayed evident embarrassment in purchasing hosiery from young ladies, to warrant putting a man clerk in one of the sections for this class of trade.

The fact of the matter was, however, that the astute buyer was never able to determine the wisdom of his plan, since Jimmy's entire time was usually occupied in waiting upon impressionable young ladies. However, inasmuch as it redounded to the profit of the department, the buyer found no fault.

Possibly if Jimmy had been almost any other type of man from what he was, his presence would not have been so flamboyantly noticeable in a hosiery department. His stature, his features, and his bronzed skin, that had lost nothing of its bronze in his month's search for work through the hot summer streets of a big city, were as utterly out of place as would have been the salient characteristics of a chorus-girl in a blacksmith-shop.

For the first week Jimmy was frightfully embarrassed, and to his natural bronze was added an almost continuous flush of mortification from the moment that he entered the department in the morning until he left it at night.

"It is a job, however," he thought, "and ten dollars is better than nothing. I can hang onto it until something better turns up."

With his income now temporarily fixed at the amount of his wages, he was forced to find a less expensive boarding-place, although at the time he had rented his room he had been quite positive that there could not be a cheaper or more undesirable habitat for man. Transportation and other considerations took him to a place on Indiana Avenue near Eighteenth Street, from whence he found he could walk to and from work, thereby saving ten cents a day. "And believe me," he cogitated, "I need the ten."

Jimmy saw little of his fellow roomers. A strange, drab lot he thought them from the occasional glimpses he had had in passings upon the dark stairway and in the gloomy halls. They appeared to be quiet, inoffensive sort of folk, occupied entirely with their own affairs. He had made no friends in the place, not even an acquaintance, nor did he care to. What leisure time he had he devoted to what he now had come to consider as his life work—the answering of blind ads in the Help Wanted columns of one morning and one evening paper—the two mediums which seemed to carry the bulk of such advertising.

For a while he had sought a better position by applying during the noon hour to such places as gave an address close enough to the department store in which he worked to permit him to make the attempt during the forty-five-minute period he was allowed for his lunch.

But he soon discovered that nine-tenths of the positions were filled before he arrived, and that in the few cases where they were not he not only failed of employment, but was usually so delayed that he was late in returning to work after noon.

By replying to blind ads evenings he could take his replies to the two newspaper offices during his lunch hour, thereby losing no great amount of time. Although he never received a reply, he still persisted as he found the attempt held something of a fascination for him, similar probably to that which holds the lottery devotee or the searcher after buried treasure—there was always the chance that he would turn up something big.

And so another month dragged by slowly. His work in the department store disgusted him. It seemed such a silly, futile occupation for a full-grown man, and he was always fearful that the sister or sweetheart or mother of some of his Chicago friends would find him there behind the counter in the hosiery section.

The store was a large one, including many departments, and Jimmy tried to persuade the hosiery buyer to arrange for his transfer to another department where his work would be more in keeping with his sex and appearance.

He rather fancied the automobile accessories line, but the buyer was perfectly satisfied with Jimmy's sales record, and would do nothing to assist in the change. The university heavyweight champion had reached a point where he loathed but one thing more than he did silk hosiery, and that one thing was himself.

6

HAROLD PLAYS THE RAVEN

MASON COMPTON, president and general manager, sat in his private office in the works of the International Machine Company, chewing upon an unlighted cigar and occasionally running his fingers through his iron-gray hair as he compared and recompared two statements which lay upon the desk before him.

"Damn strange," he muttered as he touched a button beneath the edge of his desk. A boy entered the room. "Ask Mr. Bince if he will be good enough to step in here a moment, please," said Compton; and a moment later, when Harold Bince entered, the older man leaned back in his chair and motioned the other to be seated.

"I can't understand these statements, Harold," said Compton. "Here is one for August of last year and this is this August's statement of costs. We never had a better month in the history of this organization than last month, and yet our profits are not commensurate with the volume of business that we did. That's the reason I sent for these cost statements and have compared them, and I find that our costs have increased out of all proportions to what is warranted. How do you account for it?"

"Principally the increased cost of labor," replied Bince. "The same holds true of everybody else. Every manufacturer in the country is in the same plight we are."

"I know," agreed Compton, "that that is true to some measure. Both labor and raw materials have advanced, but we have advanced our prices correspondingly. In some instances it seems to me that our advance in prices, particularly on the specialties, should have given us even a handsomer profit over the increased cost of production than we formerly received.

"In the last six months since I appointed you assistant manager I am afraid that I have sort of let things get out of my grasp. I have a lot of confidence in you, Harold, and now that you and Elizabeth are engaged I feel even more inclined to let you shoulder the responsibilities that I have carried alone from the inception of this organization. But I've got to be mighty sure that you are going to do at least as well as I did. You have shown a great deal of ability, but you are young and haven't had the advantage of the years of experience that made it possible for me to finally develop a business second to none in this line in the West.

"I never had a son, and after Elizabeth's mother died I have lived in the hope somehow that she would marry the sort of chap who would really take the place of such a son as every man dreams of —some one who will take his place and carry on his work when he is ready to lay aside his tools. I liked your father, Harold. He was one of the best friends that I ever had, and I can tell you now what I couldn't have told you a month ago: that when I employed you and put you in this position it was with the hope that eventually you would fill the place in my business and in my home of the son I never had."

"Do you think Elizabeth guessed what was in your mind?" asked Bince.

"I don't know," replied the older man. "I have tried never to say anything to influence her. Years ago when she was younger we used to talk about it half jokingly, and shortly after you told me of your engagement she remarked to me one day that she was happy, for she knew you were going to be the sort of son I had wanted.

"I haven't anybody on earth but her, Harold, and when I die she gets the business. I have arranged it in my will so that you two will share and share alike in the profits after I go, but that will be some time. I am far from being an old man, and I am a mighty healthy one. However, I should like to be relieved of the active management. There are lots of things that I have always wanted to do that I couldn't do because I couldn't spare the time from my business.

"And so I want you to get thoroughly into the harness as soon as possible, that I may turn over the entire management to you. But I can't do it, Harold, while the profits are diminishing."

As the older man's gaze fell again to the statements before him the eyes of the younger man narrowed just a trifle as they rested upon Mason

Compton, and then as the older man looked up Bince's expression changed.

"I'll do my best, sir," he said, smiling. "Of course I realize, as you must, that I have tried to learn a great deal in a short time. I think I have reached a point now where I pretty thoroughly grasp the possibilities and requirements of my work, and I am sure that from now on you will note a decided change for the better on the right side of the ledger."

"I am sure of it, my boy," said Compton heartily. "Don't think that I have been finding fault with anything you have done. I just wanted to call your attention to these figures. They mean something, and it's up to you to find out just what they do mean."

And then there came a light tap on the door, which opened immediately before any summons to enter had been given, and Elizabeth Compton entered, followed by another young woman.

"Hello, there!" exclaimed Compton. "What gets us out so early? And Harriet, too! There is only one thing that would bring you girls in here so early."

"And what's that?" asked Elizabeth.

"You are going shopping, and Elizabeth wants some money."

They all laughed.

"You're a regular Sherlock Holmes!" exclaimed Harriet Holden.

"How much?" asked Compton of his daughter, still smiling.

"How much have you?" asked Elizabeth. "I am utterly broke."

Compton turned to Bince. "Get her what she

needs, Harold," he said.

The young man started to the door.

"Come with me, Elizabeth," he said; "we will go out to the cashier's cage and get you fixed up."

They entered Bince's office, which adjoined Compton's.

"Wait here a minute, Elizabeth," said Bince. "How much do you want? I'll get it for you and bring it back. I want to see you a moment alone before you go."

She told him how much she wanted, and he was back shortly with the currency.

"Elizabeth," he said, "I don't know whether you have noticed it or not, because your father isn't a man to carry his troubles home, but I believe that he is failing rapidly, largely from overwork. He worries about conditions here which really do not exist. I have been trying to take the load off his shoulders so that he could ease up a bit, but he has got into a rut from which he cannot be guided.

"He will simply have to be lifted completely out of it, or he will stay here and die in the harness. Everything is running splendidly, and now that I have a good grasp of the business I can handle it. Don't you suppose you could persuade him to take a trip? I know that he wants to travel. He has told me so several times, and if he could get away from here this fall and stay away for a year, if possible, it would make a new man of him. I am really very much worried about him, and while I hate to worry you I feel that you are the only person who can influence him and that something ought to be done and done at once."

"Why, Harold," exclaimed the girl, "there is

nothing the matter with father! He was never better in his life nor more cheerful."

"That's the side of him that he lets you see," replied the man. "His gaiety is all forced. If you could see him after you leave you would realize that he is on the verge of a nervous breakdown. Your father is not an old man in years, but he has placed a constant surtax on his nervous system for the last twenty-five years without a let-up, and it doesn't make any difference how good a machine may be it is going to wear out some day, and the better the machine the more complete will be the wreck when the final break occurs."

As he spoke he watched the girl's face, the changing expression of it, which marked her growing mental perturbation.

"You really believe it is as bad as that, Harold?" she asked.

"It may be worse than I think," he said. "It is surely fully as bad."

The girl rose slowly from the chair. "I will try and persuade him to see Dr. Earle."

The man took a step toward her. "I don't believe a doctor is what he needs," he said quickly. "His condition is one that even a nerve specialist might not diagnose correctly. It is only some one in a position like mine, who has an opportunity to observe him almost hourly, day by day, who would realize his condition. I doubt if he has any organic trouble whatever. What he needs is a long rest, entirely free from any thought whatever of business. At least, Elizabeth, it will do him no harm, and it may prolong his life for years. I wouldn't go messing around with any of these medical chaps."

"Well," she said at last, with a sigh, "I will talk to him and see if I can't persuade him to take a trip. He has always wanted to visit Japan and China."

"Just the thing!" exclaimed Bince; "just the thing for him. The long sea voyage will do him a world of good. And now," he said, stepping to her side and putting an arm around her.

She pushed him gently away.

"No," she said; "I do not feel like kissing now," and turning she entered her father's office, followed by Bince.

7

JOBLESS AGAIN

FROM her father's works Elizabeth and Harriet drove to the shopping district, where they strolled through a couple of shops and then stopped at one of the larger stores.

Jimmy Torrance was arranging his stock, fully nine-tenths of which he could have sworn he had just shown an elderly spinster who had taken at least half an hour of his time and then left without making a purchase. His back was toward his counter when his attention was attracted by a feminine voice asking if he was busy. As he turned about he recognized her instantly—the girl for whom he had changed a wheel a month before and who unconsciously had infused new ambition into his blood and saved him, temporarily at least, from becoming a quitter.

He noticed as he waited on her that she seemed to be appraising him very carefully, and at times there was a slightly puzzled expression on her face, but evidently she did not recognize him, and finally when she had concluded her purchases he was disappointed that she paid for them in cash. He had rather hoped that she would have them charged and sent, that he might learn her name and address. And then she left, with Jimmy none the wiser concerning her other than that her first name was Elizabeth and that she was even better-looking than he recalled her to have been.

"And the girl with her!" exclaimed Jimmy mentally. "She was no slouch either. They are the two best-looking girls I have seen in this town, notwithstanding the fact that whether one likes Chicago or not he's got to admit that there are more pretty girls here than in any other city in the country.

"I'm glad she didn't recognize me. Of course, I don't know her, and the chances are that I never shall, but I should hate to have any one recognize me here, or hereafter, as that young man at the stocking-counter. Gad! but it's beastly that a regular life-sized man should be selling stockings to women for a living, or rather for a fraction of a living."

While Jimmy had always been hugely disgusted with his position, the sight of the girl seemed to have suddenly crystallized all those weeks of self-contempt into a sudden almost mad desire to escape what he considered his degrading and effeminating surroundings. One must bear with Jimmy and judge him leniently, for after all, notwithstanding his college diploma and his physique, he was still but a boy, and so while it is difficult for a mature and sober judgment to countenance his next step, if one can look back a few years to his own youth he can at least find extenuating circumstances surrounding Jimmy's seeming foolishness.

For with a bang that caused startled clerks in all directions to look up from their work he shattered the decorous monotone of the great store by slamming his salesbook viciously upon the counter, and without a word of explanation to his fellow clerks marched out of the section toward the buyer's desk.

"Well, Mr. Torrance," asked that gentleman, "what can I do for you?"

"I am going to quit," announced Jimmy.

"Quit!" exclaimed the buyer. "Why, what's wrong? Isn't everything perfectly satisfactory? You have never complained to me."

"I can't explain," replied Jimmy. "I am going to quit. I am not satisfied. I am going to—er—ah—accept another position."

The buyer raised his eyebrows. "Ah!" he said. "With——" and he named their closest competitor.

"No," said Jimmy. "I am going to get a regular he-job."

The other smiled. "If an increase in salary," he suggested, "would influence you, I had intended to tell you that I would take care of you beginning next week. I thought of making it fifteen dollars," and with that unanswerable argument for Jimmy's continued service the buyer sat back and folded his hands.

"Nothing stirring," said Jimmy. "I wouldn't sell another sock if you paid me ten thousand dollars a year. I am through."

"Oh, very well," said the buyer aggrievedly, "but

if you leave me this way you will be unable to refer to the house."

But nothing, not even a team of oxen, could have held Jimmy in that section another minute, and so he got his pay and left with nothing more in view than a slow death by starvation.

"There," exclaimed Elizabeth Compton, as she sank back on the cushions of her car.

"There what?" asked Harriet.

"I have placed him."

"Whom?"

"That nice-looking young person who waited on us in the hosiery section."

"Oh!" said Harriet. "He was nice-looking, wasn't he? But he looked out of place there, and I think he felt out of place. Did you notice how he flushed when he asked you what size?" and the girls laughed heartily at the recollection. "But where have you ever met him before?" Harriet asked.

"I have never *met* him," corrected Elizabeth, accenting the "met." "He changed a wheel on the roadster several weeks ago one evening after I had taken Harold down to the club. And he was very nice about it. I should say that he is a gentleman, although his clothes were pretty badly worn."

"Yes," said Harriet, "his suit was shabby, but his linen was clean and his coat well brushed."

"My!" exclaimed Elizabeth. "He must have made an impression on some one."

"Well," said Harriet, "it isn't often you see such a nice-looking chap in the hosiery section."

"No," said Elizabeth, "and probably if he were

as nice as he looks he wouldn't be there."

Whereupon the subject was changed, and she promptly forgot Mr. Jimmy Torrance. But Jimmy was not destined soon to forget her, for as the jobless days passed and he realized more and more what an ass he had made of himself, and why, he had occasion to think about her a great deal, although never in any sense reproaching her. He realized that the fault was his own, and that he had done a foolish thing in giving up his position because of a girl he did not know and probably never would.

There came a Saturday when Jimmy, jobless and fundless, dreaded his return to the Indiana Avenue rooming-house, where he knew the landlady would be eagerly awaiting him, for he was a week in arrears in his room rent already, and had been warned he could expect no further credit.

"There is a nice young man wanting your room," the landlady had told him, "and I shall have to be having it Saturday night unless you can pay up."

Jimmy stood on the corner of Clark and Van Buren looking at his watch. "I hate to do it," he thought, "but the Lizard said he could get twenty for it, and twenty would give me another two weeks." And so his watch went, and two weeks later his cigarette-case and ring followed. Jimmy had never gone in much for jewelry—a fact which he now greatly lamented.

Some of the clothes he still had were good, though badly in want of pressing, and when, after still further days of fruitless searching for work the proceeds from the articles he had pawned were exhausted, it occurred to him he might raise something on all but what he actually needed to cover his nakedness.

In his search for work he was still wearing his best-looking suit; the others he would dispose of; and with this plan in his mind on his return to his room that night he went to the tiny closet to make a bundle of the things which he would dispose of on the morrow, only to discover that in his absence some one had been there before him, and that there was nothing left for him to sell.

It would be two days before his room rent was again due, but in the mean time Jimmy had no money wherewith to feed the inner man. It was an almost utterly discouraged Jimmy who crawled into his bed to spend a sleepless night of worry and vain regret, the principal object of his regret being that he was not the son of a blacksmith who had taught him how to shoe horses and who at the same time had been too poor to send him to college.

Long since there had been driven into his mind the conviction that for any practical purpose in life a higher education was as useless as the proverbial fifth wheel to the coach.

"And even," mused Jimmy, "if I had graduated at the head of my class, I would be no better off than I am now."

Part Two

8

BREAD FROM THE WATERS

THE next day, worn out from loss of sleep, the young man started out upon a last frenzied search for employment. He had no money for breakfast, and so he went breakfastless, and as he had no carfare it was necessary for him to walk the seemingly interminable miles from one prospective job to another. By the middle of the afternoon Jimmy was hungrier than he had ever been before in his life. He was so hungry that it actually hurt, and he was weak from physical fatigue and from disappointment and worry.

"I've got to eat," he soliloquized fiercely, "if I have to go out to-night and pound somebody on the head to get the price, and I'm going to do it," he concluded as the odors of cooking food came to him from a cheap restaurant which he was passing. He stopped a moment and looked into the window at the catsup bottles and sad-looking pies which the proprietor apparently seemed to think formed an artistic and attractive window display.

"If I had a brick," thought Jimmy, "I would

have one of those pies, even if I went to the jug for it," but his hunger had not made him as desperate as he thought he was, and so he passed slowly on, and, glancing into the windows of the store next door, saw a display of second-hand clothes and the sign "Clothes Bought and Sold."

Jimmy looked at those in the window and then down at his own, which, though wrinkled, were infinitely better than anything on display.

"I wonder," he mused, "if I couldn't put something over in the way of high finance here," and, acting upon the inspiration, he entered the dingy little shop. When he emerged twenty minutes later he wore a shabby and rather disreputable suit of hand-me-downs, but he had two silver dollars in his pocket.

When Jimmy returned to his room that night it was with a full stomach, but with the knowledge that he had practically reached the end of his rope. He had been unable to bring himself to the point of writing his father an admission of his failure, and in fact he had gone so far, and in his estimation had sunk so low, that he had definitely determined he would rather starve to death now than admit his utter inefficiency to those whose respect he most valued.

As he climbed the stairway to his room he heard some one descending from above, and as they passed beneath the dim light of a flickering gas-jet he realized that the other stopped suddenly and turned back to look after him as Jimmy continued his ascent of the stairs; and then a low voice inquired:

"Say, bo, what you doin' here?"

Jimmy turned toward the questioner.

"Oh!" he exclaimed as recognition of the other dawned slowly upon him. "It's you, is it? My old and esteemed friend, the Lizard."

"Sure, it's me," replied the Lizard. "But what you doin' here? Looking for an assistant general manager?"

Jimmy grinned.

"Don't rub it in," he said, still smiling.

The other ascended toward him, his keen eyes appraising him from head to foot.

"You live here?" he asked.

"Yes," replied Jimmy; "do you?"

"Sure, I been livin' here for the last six months."

"That's funny," said Jimmy; "I have been here about two months myself."

"What's the matter with you?" asked the Lizard. "Didn't you like the job as general manager?"

Jimmy flushed.

"Forget it," he admonished.

"Where's you room?" asked the Lizard.

"Up another flight," said Jimmy. "Won't you come up?"

"Sure," said the Lizard, and together the two ascended the stairs and entered Jimmy's room. Under the brighter light there the Lizard scrutinized his host.

"You been against it, bo, haven't you?" he asked.

"I sure have," said Jimmy.

"Gee," said the other, "what a difference clothes make! You look like a regular bum."

"Thanks," said Jimmy.

"What you doin'?" asked the Lizard.

"Nothing."

"Lose your job?"

"I quit it," said Jimmy. "I've only worked a month since I've been here, and that for the munificent salary of ten dollars a week."

"Do you want to make some coin?" asked the Lizard.

"I sure do," said Jimmy. "I don't know of anything I would rather have."

"I'm pullin' off something to-morrow night. I can use you," and he eyed Jimmy shrewdly as he spoke.

"Cracking a box?" asked Jimmy, grinning.

"It might be something like that," replied the Lizard; "but you won't have nothin' to do but stand where I put you and make a noise like a cat if you see anybody coming. It ought to be something good. I been working on it for three months. We'll split something like fifty thousand thirty-seventy."

"Is that the usual percentage?" asked Jimmy.

"It's what I'm offerin' you," replied the Lizard.

Thirty per cent of fifty thousand dollars! Jimmy jingled the few pieces of silver remaining in his pocket. Fifteen thousand dollars! And here he had been walking his legs off and starving in a vain attempt to earn a few paltry dollars honestly.

"There's something wrong somewhere," muttered Jimmy to himself.

"I'm taking it from an old crab who has more than he can use, and all of it he got by robbing people that didn't have any to spare. He's a big guy here. When anything big is doing the newspaper guys interview him, and his name is in all the lists of subscriptions to charity—when they're going to be published in the papers. I'll bet he takes nine-tenths of his kale from women and children, and he's an honored citizen. I ain't no angel, but whatever I've taken didn't cause nobody any sufferin'—I'm a thief, bo, and I'm mighty proud of it when I think of what this other guy is."

Thirty per cent of fifty thousand dollars! Jimmy was sitting with his legs crossed. He looked down at his ill-fitting, shabby trousers, and then turned up the sole of one shoe which was worn through almost to his sock. The Lizard watched him as the cat watches a mouse. He knew that the other was thinking hard, and that presently he would reach a decision, and through Jimmy's mind marched a sordid and hateful procession of recent events—humiliation, rebuff, shame, poverty, hunger, and in the background the face of his father and the face of a girl whose name, even, he did not know.

Presently he looked up at the Lizard.

"Nothing doing, old top," he said. "But don't mistake the motives which prompt me to refuse your glittering offer. I am moved by no moral scruples, however humiliating such a confession should be. The way I feel now I would almost as lief go out and rob widows and orphans myself, but each of us, some time in our life, has to consider some one who would probably rather see us dead than disgraced. I don't know whether you get me or not."

"I get you," replied the Lizard, "and while you may never wear diamonds, you'll get more pleasure out of life than I ever will, provided you don't starve to death too soon. You know, I had a hunch you would turn me down, and I'm glad you did. If you were going crooked some time I thought I'd like to have you with me. When it comes to men, I'm a pretty good picker. That's the reason I have kept out of jail so long. I either pick a square one or I work alone."

"Thanks," said Jimmy, "but how do you know that after you pull this job I won't tip off the police and claim the reward?"

The Lizard grinned his lip grin.

"There ain't one chance in a million," he said. "You'd starve to death before you'd do it. And now, what you want is a job. I can probably get you one if you ain't too particular."

"I'd do anything," said Jimmy, "that I could do and still look a policeman in the face."

"All right," said the Lizard. "When I come back I'll bring you a job of some sort. I may be back to-night, and I may not be back again for a month, and in the mean time you got to live."

He drew a roll of bills from his pocket and commenced to count out several.

"Hold on!" cried Jimmy. "Once again, nothing doing."

"Forget it," admonished the Lizard. "I'm just payin' back the twenty you loaned me."

"But I didn't loan it to you," said Jimmy; "I gave it to you as a reward for finding my watch."

The Lizard laughed and shoved the money across the table.

"Take it," he said; "don't be a damn fool. And now, so-long! I may bring you home a job to-night, but if I don't you've got enough to live on for a couple of weeks."

After the Lizard had gone Jimmy sat looking at the twenty dollars for a long time.

"That fellow may be a thief," he soliloquized, "but whatever he is, he's white. Just imagine, the only friend I've got in Chicago is a safe-blower."

9

HAROLD SITS IN A GAME

WHEN Elizabeth Compton broached to her father the subject of a much-needed rest and a trip to the Orient, he laughed at her. "Why, girl," he cried, "I was never better in my life! Where in the world did you get this silly idea?"

"Harold noticed it first," she replied, "and called my attention to it; and now I can see that you really have been failing."

"Failing!" ejaculated Compton, with a scoff. "Failing nothing! You're a pair of young idiots. I'm good for twenty years more of hard work, but, as I told Harold, I would like to quit and travel, and I shall do so just as soon as I am convinced that he can take my place."

"Couldn't he do it now?" asked the girl.

"No, I am afraid not," replied Compton. "It is too much to expect of him, but I believe that in another year he will be able to."

And so Compton put an end to the suggestion that he travel for his health, and that night when Bince called she told him that she had been unable to persuade her father that he needed a rest.

"I am afraid," he said, "that you don't take it seriously enough yourself, and that you failed to impress upon him the real gravity of his condition. It is really necessary that he go—he must go."

The girl looked up quickly at the speaker, whose tones seemed unnecessarily vehement.

"I don't quite understand," she said, "why you should take the matter so to heart. Father is the best judge of his own condition, and, while he may need a rest, I cannot see that he is in any immediate danger."

"Oh, well," replied Bince irritably, "I just wanted him to get away for his own sake. Of course, it don't mean anything to me."

"What's the matter with you to-night, anyway, Harold?" she asked a half an hour later. "You're as cross and disagreeable as you can be."

"No, I'm not," he said. "There is nothing the matter with me at all."

But his denial failed to convince her, and as, unusually early, a few minutes later he left, she realized that she had spent a most unpleasant evening.

Bince went directly to his club, where he found four other men who were evidently awaiting him.

"Want to sit in a little game to-night, Harold?" asked one of them.

"Oh, hell," replied Bince, "you fellows have been sitting here all evening waiting for me. You know I want to. My luck's got to change some time."

"Sure thing it has," agreed another of the men.

"You certainly have been playing in rotten luck, but when it does change—oh, baby!"

As the five men entered one of the card-rooms several of the inevitable spectators drew away from the other games and approached their table, for it was a matter of club gossip that these five played for the largest stakes of any coterie among the habitués of the card-room.

It was two o'clock in the morning before Bince disgustedly threw his cards upon the table and rose. There was a nasty expression on his face and in his mind a thing which he did not dare voice—the final crystallization of a suspicion that he had long harbored, that his companions had been for months deliberately fleecing him. Tonight he had lost five thousand dollars, nor was there a man at the table who did not hold his I.O.U's. for similar amounts.

"I'm through, absolutely through," he said. "I'll be damned if I ever touch another card."

His companions only smiled wearily, for they knew that to-morrow night he would be back at the table.

"How much of old man Compton's money did you get to-night?" asked one of the four after Bince had left the room.

"About two thousand dollars," was the reply, "which, added to what I already hold, puts Mr. Compton in my debt some seven or eight thousand dollars."

Whereupon they all laughed.

"I suppose," remarked another, "that it's a damn shame, but if we don't get it some one else will."

"Is he paying anything at all?" asked another.

"Oh, yes; he comes across with something now and then, but we'll probably have to carry the bulk of it until after the wedding."

"Well, I can't carry it forever," said the first speaker. "I'm not playing here for my health," and, rising, he too left the room. Going directly to the buffet, he found Bince, as he was quite sure that he would.

"Look here, old man," he said, "I hate to seem insistent, but, on the level, I've got to have some money."

"I've told you two or three times," replied Bince, "that I'd let you have it as soon as I could get it. I can't get you any now."

"If you haven't got it, Mason Compton has," retorted the creditor; "and if you don't come across I'll go to him and get it."

Bince paled.

"You wouldn't do that, Harry?" he almost whimpered. "For God's sake, don't do that, and I'll try and see what I can do for you."

"Well," replied the other, "I don't want to be nasty, but I need some money badly."

"Give me a little longer," begged Bince, "and I'll see what I can do."

Jimmy Torrance sat a long time in thought after the Lizard left. "God!" he muttered. "I wonder what dad would say if he knew that I had come to a point where I had even momentarily considered going into partnership with a safe-blower, and that for the next two weeks I shall be compelled to subsist upon the charity of a criminal?

"I'm sure glad that I have a college education. It has helped me materially to win to my present exalted standing in society. Oh, well, I might be worse off, I suppose. At least I don't have to worry about the income tax.

"It is now October, and since the first of the year I have earned forty dollars exactly. I have also received a bequest of twenty dollars, which of course is exempt. I venture to say that there is not another able-bodied adult male in the United States the making of whose income-tax schedule would be simpler than mine."

With which philosophic trend of thought, and the knowledge that he could eat for at least two weeks longer, the erstwhile star amateur first baseman sought the doubtful comfort of his narrow, lumpy bed.

It was in the neighborhood of two o'clock the next morning that he was awakened by a gentle tapping upon the panels of his door.

"Who is it?" he asked. "What do you want?"

"It's me, bo," came the whispered reply in the unmistakable tones of the Lizard.

Jimmy arose, lighted the gas, and opened the door.

"What's the matter?" he whispered.

"Are the police on your trail?"

"No," replied the Lizard, grinning. "I just dropped in to tell you that I grabbed a job for you."

"Fine!" exclaimed Jimmy. "You're a regular fellow all right."

"As long as I can earn an honest dollar," cried

Jimmy, striking a dramatic pose, "I care not what it may be."

The Lizard's grin broadened.

"I ain't so sure about that," he said. "I know your kind. You're a regular gent. There is some honest jobs that you would just as soon have as the smallpox, and maybe this is one of them."

"What is it?" asked Jimmy. "Don't keep me guessing any longer."

"You know Feinheimer's Cabaret."

"The basement joint on Wells Street?" asked Jimmy. "Sure I know it."

"Well, that's where I got you a job," said the Lizard.

"What doing?" asked Jimmy.

"Waiter," was the reply.

"It isn't any worse than standing behind a counter selling stockings to women," said Jimmy.

"It ain't such a bad job," admitted the Lizard, "if a guy ain't too swelled up. Some of 'em make a pretty good thing out of it, what with their tips and short changing— Oh, there are lots of little ways to get yours at Feinheimer's."

"I see," said Jimmy; "but don't he pay any wages?"

"Oh, sure," replied the Lizard; "you get the union scale."

"When do I go to work?"

"Go around and see him to-morrow morning. He will put you right to work."

And so the following evening the patrons of Feinheimer's Cabaret saw a new face among the untidy servitors of the establishment—a new face and a new figure, both of which looked out of place in the atmosphere of the basement resort.

Feinheimer's Cabaret held a unique place among the restaurants of the city. Its patrons were from all classes of society. At noon its many tables were largely filled by staid and respectable business men, but at night a certain element of the underworld claimed it as their own, and there was always a sprinkling of people of the stage, artists, literary men and politicians. It was, as a certain wit described it, a social goulash, for in addition to its regular habitués there were those few who came occasionally from the upper stratum of society in the belief that they were doing something devilish. As a matter of fact, slumming parties which began and ended at Feinheimer's were of no uncommon occurrence, and as the place was more than usually orderly it was with the greatest safety that society made excursions into the underworld of crime and vice through its medium.

10

AT FEINHEIMER'S

FEINHEIMER liked Jimmy's appearance. He was big and strong, and the fact that Feinheimer always retained one or two powerful men upon his payroll accounted in a large measure for the orderliness of his place. Occasionally one might start something at Feinheimer's, but no one was ever known to finish what he started.

And so Jimmy found himself waiting upon table at a place that was both reputable and disreputable, serving business men at noon and criminals and the women of the underworld at night. In the weeks that he was there he came to know many of the local celebrities in various walks of life, to know them at least by name. There was Steve Murray, the labor leader, whom rumor said was one of Feinheimer's financial backers—a large man with a loud voice and the table manners of a Duroc-Jersey. Jimmy took an instinctive dislike to the man the first time that he saw him.

And then there was Little Eva, whose real name was Edith. She was a demure-looking little girl, who came in every afternoon at four o'clock for her breakfast. She usually came to Jimmy's table when it was vacant, and at four o'clock she always ate alone. Later in the evening she would come in again with a male escort, who was never twice the same.

"I wonder what's the matter with me?" she said to Jimmy one day as he was serving her breakfast. "I'm getting awfully nervous."

"That's quite remarkable," said Jimmy. "I should think any one who smoked as many cigarettes and drank as much whisky as you would have perfect nerves."

The girl laughed, a rather soft and mellow laugh. "I suppose I do hit it up a little strong," she said.

"Strong?" exclaimed Jimmy. "Why, if I drank half what you do I'd be in the Washingtonian Home in a week."

She looked at him quizzically for a moment, as she had looked at him often since he had gone to work for Feinheimer.

"You're a funny guy," she said. "I can't quite figure you out. What are you doing here anyway?"

"I never claimed to be much of a waiter," said Jimmy, "but I didn't know I was so rotten that a regular customer of the place couldn't tell what I was trying to do."

"Oh, go on," she cried; "I don't mean that. These other hash-slingers around here look the part. Aside from that, about the only thing they know how to do is roll a souse; but you're different."

"Yes," said Jimmy, "I am different. My abilities

are limited. All I can do is wait on table, while they have two accomplishments."

"Oh, you don't have to tell me," said the girl. "I wasn't rubbering. I was just sort of interested in you."

"Thanks," said Jimmy.

She went on with her breakfast while Jimmy set up an adjoining table. Presently when he came to fill her water-glass she looked up at him again.

"I like you, kid," she said. "You're not fresh. You know what I am as well as the rest of them, but you wait on me just the same as you would on" —she hesitated and there was a little catch in her voice as she finished her sentence—"just the same as you would on a decent girl."

Jimmy looked at her in surprise. It was the first indication that he had ever had from an habitué of Feinheimer's that there might lurk within their breasts any of the finer characteristics whose outward indices are pride and shame. He was momentarily at a loss as to what to say, and as he hesitated the girl's gaze went past him and she exclaimed:

"Look who's here!"

Jimmy turned to look at the newcomer, and saw the Lizard directly behind him.

"Howdy, bo," said his benefactor. "I thought I'd come in and give you the once-over. And here's Little Eva with a plate of ham and at four o'clock in the afternoon."

The Lizard dropped into a chair at the table with the girl, and after Jimmy had taken his order and departed for the kitchen Little Eva jerked her thumb toward his retreating figure.

"Friend of yours?" she asked.

"He might have a worse friend," replied the Lizard non-committally.

"What's his graft?" asked the girl.

"He ain't got none except being on the square. It's funny," the Lizard philosophized, "but here's me with a bank roll that would choke a horse, and you probably with a stocking full of dough, and I'll bet all the money I ever had or ever expect to have if one of us could change places with that poor simp we'd do it."

"He is a square guy, isn't he?" said the girl. "You can almost tell it by looking at him. How did you come to know him?"

"Oh, that's a long story," said the Lizard. "We room at the same place, but I knew him before that."

"On Indiana near Eighteenth?" asked the girl.

"How the hell did you know?" he queried.

"I know a lot of things I ain't supposed to know," replied she.

"You're a wise guy, all right, Eva, and one thing I like about you is that you don't let anything you know hurt you."

And then, after a pause: "I like him," she said. "What's his name?"

The Lizard eyed her for a moment.

"Don't you get to liking him too much," he said. "That bird's the class. He ain't for any little—"

"Cut it!" exclaimed the girl. "I'm as good as you are and a damn sight straighter. What I get I earn, and I don't steal it."

The Lizard grinned. "I guess you're right at that;

but don't try to pull him down any lower than he is. He is coming up again some day to where he belongs."

"I ain't going to try to pull him down," said the girl. "And anyhow, when were you made his godfather?"

Jimmy saw Eva almost daily for many weeks. He saw her at her post-meridian breakfast, sober and subdued; he saw her later in the evening, in various stages of exhilaration, but at those times she did not come to his table and seldom if ever did he catch her eye.

They talked a great deal while she breakfasted, and he learned to like the girl and to realize that she possessed two personalities. The one which he liked dominated her at breakfast; the other which he loathed guided her actions later in the evening. Neither of them ever referred to those hours of her life, and as the days passed Jimmy found himself looking forward to the hour when Little Eva would come to Feinheimer's for her breakfast.

11

CHRISTMAS EVE

IT was Christmas Eve. Elizabeth Compton and Harriet Holden were completing the rounds of their friends' homes with Christmas remembrances—a custom that they had continued since childhood. The last parcel had been delivered upon the South Side, and they were now being driven north on Michigan Boulevard toward home. Elizabeth directed the chauffeur to turn over Van Buren to State, which at this season of the year was almost alive with belated Christmas shoppers and those other thousands who always seize upon the slightest pretext for a celebration.

It was a noisy, joyous crowd whose spirit, harmonizing with the bright lights and the gay shop windows, infected all who came within its influence. As the car moved slowly northward along the world's greatest retail street the girls leaned forward to watch the passing throng through the windows.

"Isn't it wonderful," exclaimed Harriet, "what a transformation a few lights make? Who would ever think of State Street as a fairy-land? And yet, if you half close your eyes, the hallucination is complete. Even the people who by daylight are shoddy and care-worn take on an appearance of romance and gaiety, and the tawdry colored lights are the scintillant gems of the garden of a fairy prince."

"Don't!" Elizabeth pleaded. "The city at night always affects me. It makes me want to do something adventurous, and on Christmas Eve it is even worse. If you keep on like that I shall soon be telling David to drive us up and down State Street all night."

"I wish we didn't have to go home right away," said Harriet. "I feel like doing something devilish."

"Well, let's!" exclaimed Elizabeth.

"Do something devilish?" inquired Harriet. "What, for instance?"

"Oh, 'most anything that we shouldn't do," replied Elizabeth, "and there isn't anything that we could do down here alone that we should do."

They both laughed. "I have it!" exclaimed Elizabeth suddenly. "We'll be utterly abandoned—we'll have supper at Feinheimer's without an escort."

Harriet cast a horrified glance at her companion. "Why, Elizabeth Compton," she cried, "you wouldn't dare. You know you wouldn't dare!"

"Do you dare me?" asked the other.

"But suppose some one should see us?" argued

Harriet. "Your father would never forgive us."

"If we see any one in Feinheimer's who knows us," argued Elizabeth shrewdly, "they will be just as glad to forget it as we. And anyway it will do no harm. I shall have David stay right outside the door so that if I call him he can come. I don't know what I would do without David. He is a sort of Rock of Ages and Gibraltar all in one."

Through the speaking-tube Elizabeth directed David to drive to Feinheimer's, and, whatever David may have thought of the order, he gave no outward indication of it.

Christmas Eve at Feinheimer's is, or was, a riot of unconfined hilarity, although the code of ethics of the place was on a higher plane than that which governed the Christmas Eve and New Year's Eve patrons of so-called respectable restaurants, where a woman is not safe from insult even though she be properly escorted, while in Feinheimer's a woman with an escort was studiously avoided by the other celebrators unless she chose to join with them. As there was only one class of women who came to Feinheimer's at night without escort, the male habitués had no difficulty in determining who they might approach and who they might not.

Jimmy Torrance was as busy as a cranberry merchant. He had four tables to attend to, and while the amount of food he served grew more and more negligible as the evening progressed, his trips to the bar were exceeding frequent. One of his tables had been vacated for a few minutes when, upon his return from the bar with a round of drinks for Steve Murray and his party, he saw that two women had entered and were occupying his fourth table. Their backs were toward him, and he gave them but little attention other than to note that they were unescorted and to immediately catalogue them accordingly. Having distributed Steve Murray's order, Jimmy turned toward his new patrons, and, laying a menu card before each, he stood between them waiting for their order.

"What shall we take?" asked Elizabeth of Harriet. Then: "What have you that's good?" and she looked up at the waiter.

Jimmy prided himself upon self-control, and his serving at Feinheimer's had still further schooled him in the repression of any outward indication of his emotions. For, as most men of his class, he had a well-defined conception of what constituted a perfect waiter, one of the requisites being utter indifference to any of the affairs of his patrons outside of those things which actually pertained to his duties as a servitor; but in this instance Jimmy realized that he had come very close to revealing the astonishment which he felt on seeing this girl in Feinheimer's and unescorted.

If Jimmy was schooled in self-control, Elizabeth Compton was equally so. She recognized the waiter immediately, but not even by a movement of an eyelid did she betray the fact; which may possibly be accounted for by the fact that it meant little more to her than as though she had chanced to see the same street-sweeper several times in succession, although after he had left with their order she asked Harriet if she, too, had recognized him.

"Immediately," replied her friend. "It doesn't

seem possible that such a good-looking chap should be occupying such a menial position."

"There must be something wrong with him," rejoined Elizabeth; "probably utterly inefficient."

"Or he may have some vice," suggested Harriet.

"He doesn't look it," said Elizabeth. "He looks too utterly healthy for that. We've seen some of these drug addicts in our own set, as you may readily recall. No, I shouldn't say that he was that."

"I suppose the poor fellow has never had an opportunity," said Harriet. "He has a good face, his eyes and forehead indicate intelligence, and his jaw is strong and aggressive. Probably, though, he was raised in poverty and knows nothing better than what he is doing now. It is too bad that some of these poor creatures couldn't have the advantages of higher education."

"Yes," said Elizabeth, "it is too bad. Take a man like that; with a college education he could attain almost any degree of success he chose."

"He certainly could," agreed Harriet; and then suddenly: "Why, what's the matter, Elizabeth? Your face is perfectly scarlet."

The other girl tapped the floor with the toe of one boot impatiently.

"That horrid creature at the next table just winked at me," she said disgustedly.

Harriet looked about in the direction her companion had indicated, to see a large, overdressed man staring at them. There was a smirk on his face, and as Harriet caught his eye she saw him rise and, to her horror, realized that he was advancing toward their table.

He stopped in front of them with his huge hands resting on the edge of their table and looked down at Elizabeth.

"Hello, kiddo!" he said. "What are you going to drink?"

Elizabeth gave the man one look such as would utterly have frozen a male from her own stratum of society, but it had as little effect upon Steve Murray's self-assurance as the cork from a popgun would have on the armored sides of a rhinoceros.

"All right," said the man, "what's the use of asking? There's only one thing when Steve Murray buys. Here, waiter," he yelled, pounding on the table. The nearest waiter, who chanced not to be Jimmy, who was then in the kitchen, came hurriedly forward. "Open up some wine," commanded Murray. "Come on, boys! Bring your chairs over here," he continued, addressing his companions; "let's have a little party."

Elizabeth Compton rose.

"You will oblige me," she said, "by leaving our table."

Steve Murray laughed uproariously. He had dropped into a chair next to hers.

"That's great!" he cried. "I guess you don't know who I am, kiddo. You won't cop off anything better in this joint than Steve Murray. Come on—let's be friends. That's a good girl," and before Elizabeth realized the man's intentions he had seized her wrist and pulled her down into his lap.

It was this scene that broke upon Jimmy's view as he emerged from the kitchen with a laden tray.

He saw Steve Murray seize the girl, and he saw her struggling to free herself, and then there was a mighty crash as Jimmy dropped the tray of steaming food upon the floor and ran quickly forward.

Murray was endeavoring to draw the girl's lips to his as Jimmy's hand shot between their faces and pushed that of the man away. With his free arm he encircled the girl's body and attempted to draw her from her assailant.

"Cut it, Murray!" he commanded in a low tone of voice. "She isn't your sort."

"Who the hell are you?" cried the labor leader, releasing the girl and rising to his feet. "Get the hell out of here, you dirty hash-slinger! Any girl in this place belongs to me if I want her. There don't only one kind come in here without an escort, or with one, either, for that matter. You get back on your job, where you belong," and the man pressed forward trying to push Jimmy aside and lay hands on Elizabeth again.

Jimmy did not strike him then. He merely placed the palm of one hand against the man's breast and pushed him backward, but with such force that, striking a chair, Steve Murray fell backward and sprawled upon the floor. Scrambling to his feet, he rushed Jimmy like a mad bull.

In his younger days Murray had been a boilermaker, and he still retained most of his great strength. He was a veritable mountain of a man, and now in the throes of a berserker rage he was a formidable opponent. His face was white and his lips were drawn back tightly, exposing his teeth in a bestial snarl as he charged at Jimmy. His great arms and huge hands beat to the right and left like enormous flails, one blow from which might seemingly have felled an ox.

Torrance had stood for a moment with an arm still around the girl; but as Murray rose to his feet he pushed her gently behind him, and then as the man was upon him Jimmy ducked easily under the other's clumsy left and swung a heavy right hook to his jaw. As Murray staggered to the impact of the blow Jimmy reached him again quickly and easily with a left to the nose, from which a crimson burst spattered over the waiter and his victim. Murray went backward and would have fallen but for the fact he came in contact with one of his friends, and then he was at Jimmy again.

By this time waiters and patrons were crowding forward from all parts of the room, and Feinheimer, shrieking at the top of his voice, was endeavoring to worm his fat, toadlike body through the cordon of excited spectators. The proprietor reached the scene of carnage just in time to see Jimmy plant a lovely left on the point of Murray's jaw.

The big man tottered drunkenly for an instant, his knees sagged, and, as Jimmy stood in readiness for any eventuality, the other crashed heavily to the floor.

Towering above the others in the room suddenly came a big young fellow shouldering his way through the crowd, a young man in the uniform of a chauffeur. Elizabeth saw him before he discovered her.

"Oh, David!" she cried. "Quick! Quick! Take us out of here!"

As the chauffeur reached her side and took in the

scene he jerked his head toward Jimmy. "Did any one hurt you, miss?"

"No, no!" she cried. "This man was very kind. Just get us out of here, David, as quickly as you can." And, turning to Jimmy: "How can I ever repay you? If it hadn't been for you—oh, I hate to think what would have happened. Come out to the car and give David your name and address, and I will send you something tomorrow."

"Oh, that's all right," said Jimmy. "You just get out of here as quick as you can. If the police happened to look in now you might be held as a witness."

"How utterly horrible!" exclaimed Elizabeth. "Come, David! Come, Harriet!" David making a way for her, she started for the door.

Harriet paused long enough to extend her hand to Jimmy. "It was wonderfully brave of you," she said. "We could never do enough to repay you. My name is Harriet Holden," and she gave him an address on Lake Shore Drive. "If you will come Monday morning about ten o'clock," she said, "I am sure that there is something we can do for you. If you want a better position," she half suggested, "I know my father could help, although he must never know about this to-night."

"Thanks," said Jimmy, smiling. "It's awfully good of you, but you must hurry now. There goes your friend."

Feinheimer stood as one dazed, looking down at the bulk of his friend and associate.

"Mein Gott!" he cried. "What kind of a place you think I run, young man?" He turned angrily on

Jimmy. "What you think I hire you for? To beat up my best customer?"

"He got what was coming to him," said a soft feminine voice at Jimmy's elbow. The man looked to see Little Eva standing at his side. "I didn't think anybody could do that to Murray," she continued. "Lord, but it was pretty. He's had it coming to him ever since I've known him, but the big stiff had everybody around this joint buffaloed. He got away with anything he started."

Feinheimer looked at Little Eva disgustedly.

"He's my best customer," he cried, "and a bum waiter comes along and beats him up just when he is trying to have a little innocent sport on Christmas Eve. You take off your apron, young man, and get your time. I won't have no rough stuff in Feinheimer's."

Jimmy shrugged his shoulders and grinned.

"Shouldn't I wait to see if I can't do something more for Mr. Murray?" he suggested.

"You get out of here!" cried Feinheimer. "Get out of here or I'll call the police."

Jimmy laughed and took off his apron as he walked back to the servants' coat-room. As he emerged again and crossed through the dining-room he saw that Murray had regained consciousness and was sitting at a table wiping the blood from his face with a wet napkin. As Murray's eyes fell upon his late antagonist he half rose from his chair and shook his fist at Jimmy.

"I'll get you for this, young feller!" he yelled. "I'll get you yet, and don't you forget it."

"You just had me," Jimmy called back; "but it

didn't seem to make you very happy."

He could still hear Murray fuming and cursing as he passed out into the barroom, at the front of which was Feinheimer's office.

12

UP OR DOWN?

AFTER Jimmy had received his check and was about to leave, a couple of men approached him.

"We seen that little mix-up in there," said one of them. "You handle your mitts like you been there before."

"Yes," said Jimmy, smiling, "I've had a little experience in the manly art of self-defense."

The two men were sizing him up.

"Feinheimer can you?" asked one of them. Jimmy nodded affirmatively. "Got anything else in view?"

"No," said Jimmy.

"How'd you like a job as one of Brophy's sparring partners?"

"I wouldn't mind," said Jimmy. "What is there in it?"

They named a figure that was entirely satisfactory to Jimmy.

"Come over the day after Christmas," he was told, "and we'll give you a trial."

"I wonder," thought Jimmy as he started for

home, "if I have gone up a notch in the social scale or down a notch? From the view-point of the underworld a pug occupies a more exalted position than a waiter; but—oh, well, a job's a job, and at least I won't have to look at that greasy Feinheimer all day."

At ten o'clock Monday Jimmy was at Young Brophy's training quarters, for, although he had not forgotten Harriet Holden's invitation, he had never seriously considered availing himself of her offer to help him to a better position. While he had not found it difficult to accept the rough friendship and assistance of the Lizard, the idea of becoming an object of "charity," as he considered it, at the hands of a girl in the same walk of life as that to which he belonged was intolerable.

Young Brophy's manager, whom Jimmy discovered to be one of the men who had accosted him in Feinheimer's after his trouble with Murray, took him into a private office and talked with him confidentially for a half-hour before he was definitely employed.

It seemed that one of the principal requisites of the position was a willingness to take punishment without attempting to inflict too much upon Young Brophy. The manager did not go into specific details as to the reason for this restriction, and Jimmy, badly in need of a job, felt no particular inclination to search too deeply for the root of the matter.

"What I don't know," he soliloquized, "won't hurt me any." But he had not been there many days before the piecing together of chance remarks and the gossip of the hangers-on and other sparring partners made it very apparent why Brophy should not be badly man-handled. As it finally revealed itself to Jimmy it was very simple indeed. Brophy was to be pitted against a man whom he had already out-pointed in a former bout. He was the ruling favorite in the betting, and it was the intention to keep him so while he and his backers quietly placed all their money on the other man.

One of the sparring partners who seemed to harbor a petty grudge against Brophy finally explained the whole plan to Jimmy. Everything was to be done to carry the impression to the public through the newspapers, who were usually well represented at the training quarters, that Brophy was in the pink of condition; that he was training hard; that it was impossible to find men who could stand up to him on account of the terrific punishment he inflicted upon his sparring partners; and that the result of the fight was already a foregone conclusion; and then in the third round Young Brophy was to lie down and by reclining peacefully on his stomach for ten seconds make more money than several years of hard and conscientious work earnestly performed could ever net him.

It was all very, very simple; but how easily public opinion might be changed should one of the sparring partners really make a good stand against Brophy in the presence of members of the newspaper fraternity!

"I see," said Jimmy, running his fingers through his hair. "Oh, well, it's none of my business, and if the suckers want to bet their money on a prize-fight they're about due to lose it anyway."

And so he continued permitting himself to be battered up four or five times a week at the hands of the pussy Mr. Brophy. He paid back the twenty the Lizard had loaned him, got his watch out of pawn, and was even figuring on a new suit of clothes. Never before in his life had Jimmy realized what it meant to be prosperous, since for obvious reasons Young Brophy's manager was extremely liberal in the matter of salaries with all those connected with the training-camp.

At first it had been rather humiliating to Jimmy to take the drubbings he did at the hands of Young Brophy in the presence of the audience which usually filled the small gymnasium where the fighter was training. It was nearly always about the same crowd, however, made up of dyed-in-the-wool fans, a few newspaper men, and a sprinkling of thrill-seekers from other walks of life far removed from the prize-ring. Jimmy often noticed women among the spectators—well-dressed women, with every appearance of refinement, and there were always men of the same upper class of society.

He mentioned the fact once to the same young man who had previously explained the plan under which the fight was to be faked.

"That's just part of the graft," said his informant. "These birds have got next to a bunch of would-be sports with more money than brains through the athletic director of"—he mentioned the name of one of the big athletic clubs—"and they been inviting 'em here to watch Brophy training. Every one of the simps will be tryin' to get money down on Brophy, and this bunch will take it all up as fast as they come.

"The bettin' hasn't really started yet; in fact, they are holding off themselves until the odds are better. If Brophy goes into the ring a three-to-one favorite these fellows will make a killing that will be talked of for the next twenty years."

"And incidentally give boxing another black eye," interjected Jimmy.

"Oh, what the hell do we care?" said the other. "I'm goin' to make mine out of it, and you better do the same. I'm goin' to put up every cent I can borrow or steal on the other guy."

It was Saturday, the 15th of January, just a week before the fight, that Jimmy, trained now almost to perfection, stepped into the ring to take his usual mauling. For some time past there had been insidiously working its way into his mind a vast contempt for the pugilistic prowess of Young Brophy.

"If," thought Jimmy, "this bird is of championship caliber, I might be a champion myself." For, though Young Brophy was not a champion, the newspapers had been pointing to him for some time as a likely possibility for these pugilistic honors later.

As this mental attitude grew within him and took hold of Jimmy it more and more irked him to take the punishment which he inwardly felt he could easily inflict upon Brophy instead, but, as Jimmy had learned through lean and hungry months, a job is a job, and no job is to be sneezed at or lightly thrown aside.

There was quite a gathering that afternoon to

watch Young Brophy's work-out, and rather a larger representation than usual from society's younger set. The program, which had consisted in part of shadow boxing and bag punching by Young Brophy, was to terminate with three rounds with Jimmy.

For two rounds the young man had permitted Brophy to make a monkey of him, hitting him where he would at will, while Jimmy, as a result of several weeks of diligent practise, was able to put up apparently a very ferocious attempt to annihilate his opponent without doing the latter any material damage.

At the close of the second round Brophy landed a particularly vicious right, which dropped Jimmy to the canvas. The crowd applauded vociferously, and as the gong sounded as Jimmy was slowly rising to his feet they were all assured that it was all that had saved the young man from an even worse thrashing.

As Jimmy returned to his corner there arose within him a determination to thrash Young Brophy within an inch of his life after the big fight was out of the way and Jimmy no longer bound by any obligations, for he realized that for some reason Brophy had just gone a little too far with his rough tactics, there having been in the arrangement with the sparring partners an understanding that when a knock-down was to be staged Brophy was to give his opponent the cue. No cue had been given, however. Jimmy had not been expecting it, and he had been floored with a punch behind which were all the weight and brawn of the pugilist.

He had long since ceased to consider what the spectators might think. So far as Jimmy was concerned, they might have been so many chairs. He was merely angry at the unnecessary punishment that had been inflicted. As he sprawled in his corner he let his eyes run over the faces of the spectators directly in front of him, to whom previously he had paid no particular attention, and even now it was scarcely more than an involuntary glance; but his eyes stopped suddenly upon a face, and as recognition suddenly dawned upon him he could feel the hot blood rushing to his own. For there was the girl whom Fate had thrice before thrown in his path! Beside her he recognized the Miss Harriet Holden who had been with her the night at Feinheimer's, and with them were two young men.

Something within Jimmy Torrance rebelled to a point where it utterly dominated him—rebelled at the thought that this girl, whom he had unconsciously set upon a pedestal to worship from afar, should always find him in some menial and humiliating position. It was bad enough that she should see him as a sparring partner of a professional pug, but it made it infinitely worse that she should see him as what he must appear, an unsuccessful third or fourth rate fighter.

Everything within Jimmy's mind turned suddenly topsyturvy. He seemed to lose all sense of proportion and all sense of value in one overpowering thought, that he must not again be humiliated in her presence.

And so it was that at the tap of the gong for the third round it was not Torrance the sparring partner that advanced from his corner, but Jimmy Torrance, champion heavyweight boxer of a certain famous university. But why enter into the harrowing details of the ensuing minute and a half?

In thirty seconds it was unquestionably apparent to every one in the room, including Young Brophy himself, that the latter was pitifully outclassed. Jimmy hit him whenever and wherever he elected to hit him, and he hit him hard, while Brophy, at best only a second or third rate fighter, pussy and undertrained, was not only unable to elude the blows of his adversary but equally so to land effectively himself.

And there before the eyes of half a dozen newspaper reporters, of a dozen wealthy young men who had fully intended to place large sums on Brophy, and before the eyes of his horrified manager and backer, Jimmy, at the end of ninety seconds, landed a punch that sent the flabby Mr. Brophy through the ropes and into dreamland for a much longer period than the requisite ten seconds.

Before Jimmy got dressed and out of the gymnasium he, with difficulty, escaped a half-dozen more fistic encounters, as everybody from the manager down felt that his crime deserved nothing short of capital punishment. He had absolutely wrecked a perfectly good scheme in the perfection of which several thousand dollars had been spent, and now there could not be even the possibility of a chance of their breaking even.

13

HARRIET PHILOSOPHIZES

WHEN Jimmy got home that night he saw a light in the Lizard's room and entered.

"Well," said the cracksman, "how's every little thing?"

Jimmy smiled ruefully.

"Canned again," he announced, and then he told the Lizard the story of his downfall, attributing the results of the third round, however, to Brophy's unwarranted action at the end of the second.

"Well," said the Lizard, "you certainly are the champion boob. There you had a chance to cop off a nice bunch of coin on that fight and instead you kill it for yourself and everybody else."

"You don't think," said Jimmy, "that I would have put any money on that crooked scrap."

"Why not?" asked the Lizard, and then he shook his head sadly. "No, I don't suppose you would. There's lots of things about you that I can't understand, and one of them is the fact that you would rather starve to death than take a little easy money off of birds that have got more than they got any business to have. Why, with your education and front we two could pull off some of the classiest stuff that this burg ever saw."

"Forget it," admonished Jimmy.

"What are you going to do now?" asked the Lizard.

"Go out and hunt for another job," said Jimmy.

"Well, I wish you luck," said the Lizard. "Maybe I can find something for you. I'll try, and in the mean time if you need any mazuma I always got a little roll tucked away in my sock."

"Thanks," said Jimmy, "and I don't mind telling you that you're the one man I know whom I'd just as soon borrow from and would like the opportunity of loaning to. You say that you can't understand me, and yet you're a whole lot more of an enigma yourself! You admit, in fact, you're inclined to boast, that you're a pickpocket and a safe-blower, and yet I'd trust you, Lizard, with anything that I had."

The Lizard smiled, and for the first time since he had known him Jimmy noticed that his eyes smiled with his lips.

"I've always had the reputation," said the Lizard, "of being a white guy with my friends. As a matter of fact, I ain't no different from what you'd probably be if you were in business and what most of your friends are. Morally they're a bunch of thieves and crooks. Of course, they don't go out and frisk any one and they don't work with a jimmy or a bottle of soup. They work their graft with the help of contracts and lawyers, and they'd gyp a friend or a pauper almost as soon as they would an enemy. I don't know much about morality, but when it comes right down to a question of morals I believe my trade is just as decent as that of a lot of these birds you see rolling up and down Mich Boul in their limousines."

"It's all in the point of view," said Jimmy.

"Yes," said the Lizard. "It's all in the point of view, and my point of view ain't warped by no college education."

Jimmy grinned. "Eventually, Lizard, you may win me over; but when you do why fritter away our abilities upon this simple village when we have the capitals of all Europe to play around in?"

"There's something in that," said the Lizard; "but don't get it into your head for a minute that I am tryin' to drag you from the straight and narrow. I think I like you better the way you are."

"Did you ever," said Harriet Holden, "see anything so weird as the way we keep bumping into that stocking-counter young man?"

"No," said Elizabeth, "it is commencing to get on my nerves. Every time I turn a corner now I expect to bump into him. I suppose we see other people many times without recognizing them, but he is so utterly good-looking that he sort of sticks in one's memory."

"Do you know," said Harriet, "that I have a suspicion that he recognized us. I saw him looking up at us just after that other person knocked him down and I could have sworn that he blushed. And then, you know, he went in and was entirely different from what he had been in the two preceding rounds. Billy said that he is really a wonderful fighter, and there are not very many good fights that Billy misses. What in the world do you suppose his profession is anyway? Since we first noticed him he has been a hosiery clerk, a waiter, and a prize-fighter."

"I don't know, I am sure," said Elizabeth, yawning. "You seem to be terribly interested in him."

"I am," admitted Harriet frankly. "He's a regular adventure all in himself—a whole series of adventures."

"I've never been partial to serials," said Elizabeth.

"Well, I should think one would be a relief after a whole winter of heavy tragedy," retorted Harriet.

"What do you mean?" asked Elizabeth.

"Oh, I mean Harold, of course," said Harriet. "He's gone around all winter with a grouch and a face a mile long. What's the matter with him anyway?"

"I don't know," sighed Elizabeth. "I'm afraid he's working too hard."

Harriet giggled.

"Oh, fiddlesticks!" she exclaimed. "You know perfectly well that Harold Bince will never work himself to death."

"Well, he *is* working hard, Harriet. Father says so. And he's worrying about the business, too. He's trying so hard to make good."

"I will admit that he has stuck to his job more faithfully than anybody expected him to."

Elizabeth turned slowly upon her friend.

"You don't like Harold," she said; "why is it?"
Harriet shook her head.

"I do like him, Elizabeth, for your sake. I suppose the trouble is that I realize that he is not good enough for you. I have known him all my life, and even as a little child he was never sincere. Possibly he has changed now. I hope so. And then again I know as well as you do that you are not in love with him."

"How perfectly ridiculous!" cried Elizabeth. "Do you suppose that I would marry a man whom I didn't love?"

"You haven't the remotest idea what love is. You've never been in love."

"Have you?" asked Elizabeth.

"No," replied Harriet, "I haven't, but I know the symptoms and you certainly haven't got one of them. Whenever Harold isn't going to be up for dinner or for the evening you're always relieved. Possibly you don't realize it yourself, but you show it to any one who knows you."

"Well, I do love him," insisted Elizabeth, "and I intend to marry him. I never had any patience with this silly, love-sick business that requires people to pine away when they are not together and bore everybody else to death when they were."

"All of which proves," said Harriet, "that you haven't been stung yet, and I sincerely hope that you may never be unless it happens before you marry Harold."

14

IN AGAIN—OUT AGAIN

JIMMY TORRANCE was out of a job a week this time, and once more he was indebted to the Lizard for a position, the latter knowing a politician who was heavily interested in a dairy company, with the result that Jimmy presently found himself driving a milk-wagon. Jimmy's route was on the north side, which he regretted, as it was in the district where a number of his friends of his former life resided. His delivery schedule, however, and the fact that his point of contact with the homes of his customers was at the back door relieved him of any considerable apprehension of being discovered by an acquaintance.

His letters home were infrequent, for he found that his powers of invention were being rapidly depleted. It was difficult to write glowing accounts of the business success he was upon the point of achieving on the strength of any of the positions he so far had held, and doubly so during the far greater period that he had been jobless and hungry. But he had not been able to bring himself to the point of admitting to his family his long weeks of consistent and unrelieved failure.

Recently he had abandoned his futile attempts to obtain positions through the medium of the Help Wanted columns.

"It is no use," he thought. "There must be something inherently wrong with me that in a city full of jobs I am unable to land anything without some sort of a pull and then only work that any unskilled laborer could perform."

The truth of the matter was that Jimmy Torrance was slowly approaching that mental condition that is aptly described by the phrase, "losing your grip," one of the symptoms of which was the fact that he was almost contented with his present job.

He had driven for about a week when, upon coming into the barn after completing his morning delivery, he was instructed to take a special order to a certain address on Lake Shore Drive. Although the address was not that of one of his regular customers he felt that there was something vaguely familiar about it, but when he finally arrived he realized that it was a residence at which he had never before called.

Driving up the alley Jimmy stopped in the rear of a large and pretentious home, and entering through a gateway in a high stone wall he saw that the walk to the rear entrance bordered a very delightful garden. He realized what a wonderfully pretty little spot it must be in the summer time, with its pool and fountain and tree-shaded benches, its vine-covered walls and artistically arranged shrubs, and it recalled to Jimmy with an accompanying sigh the homes in which he had visited in what seemed now a remote past, and also of his own home in the West.

On the alley in one corner of the property stood a garage and stable, in which Jimmy could see men working upon the owner's cars and about the box-stalls of his saddle horses. At the sight of the horses Jimmy heaved another sigh as he continued his way to the rear entrance. As he stood waiting for a reply to his summons he glanced back at the stable to see that two horses had just entered and that their riders were dismounting, evidently two of the women of the household, and then a houseman opened the door and Jimmy made his delivery and started to retrace his steps to his wagon.

Approaching him along the walk from the stable were the riders—two young women, laughing and talking as they approached the house, and suddenly Jimmy, in his neat white suit, carrying his little tray of milk-bottles, recognized them, and instantly there flashed into recollection the address that Harriet Holden had given him that night at Feinheimer's.

"What infernal luck," he groaned inwardly; "I suppose the next time I see that girl I'll be collecting garbage from her back door." And then, with his eyes straight to the front, he stepped aside to let the two pass.

It was Harriet Holden who recognized him first, and stopped with a little exclamation of surprise. Jimmy stopped, too. There was nothing else that a gentleman might do, although he would have given his right hand to have been out of the yard.

"You never came to the house as I asked you to," said Miss Holden reproachfully. "We wanted so much to do something to repay you for your protection that night."

"There was no use in my coming," said Jimmy, "for, you see, I couldn't have accepted anything for what I did—I couldn't very well have done anything else, could I, under the circumstances?"

"There were many other men in the place," replied Harriet, "but you were the only one who came to our help."

"But the others were not—" Jimmy had been upon the point of saying gentlemen, but then he happened to think that in the eyes of these two girls, and according to their standard, he might not be a gentleman, either. "Well, you see," he continued lamely, "they probably didn't know who you were."

"Did you?" asked Elizabeth.

"No," Jimmy admitted, "of course, I didn't know who you were, but I knew what you were not, which was the thing that counted most then."

"I wish," said Harriet, "that you would let us do something for you."

"Yes," said Elizabeth, "if a hundred dollars would be of any use to you—" Harriet laid a hand quickly on her friend's arm.

"I wasn't thinking of money," she said to Jimmy. "One can't pay for things like that with money, but we know so many people here we might help you in some way if you are not entirely satisfied with your present position."

Out of the corner of his eye Jimmy could not help but note that Elizabeth was appraising him critically from head to foot, and he felt that he could almost read what was passing through her mind as she took stock of his cheap cotton uniform and his cap, with the badge of his employer above the vizor. Involuntarily Jimmy straightened his shoulders and raised his chin a trifle.

"No, thank you," he said to Harriet, "it is kind of you, but really I am perfectly satisfied with my present job. It is by far the best one I have ever held," and touching his cap, he continued his interrupted way to his wagon.

"What a strange young man," exclaimed Harriet.

"He is like many of his class," replied Elizabeth, "probably entirely without ambition and with no desire to work any too hard or to assume additional responsibilities."

"I don't believe it," retorted Harriet. "Unless I am greatly mistaken, that man is a gentleman. Everything about him indicates it; his inflection even is that of a well-bred man."

"How utterly silly," exclaimed Elizabeth. "You've heard him speak scarcely a dozen words. I venture to say that in a fifteen-minute conversation he would commit more horrible crimes against the king's English than even that new stable-boy of yours. Really, Harriet, you seem very much interested in this person."

"Why shouldn't I be?" asked Harriet. "He's becoming my little pet mystery. I wonder under what circumstances we shall see him next?"

"Probably as a white-wings," laughed Elizabeth. "But if so I positively refuse to permit you to stop in the middle of Michigan Boulevard and converse with a street-sweeper while I'm with you."

Jimmy's new job lasted two weeks, and then the milk-wagon drivers went on strike and Jimmy was thrown out of employment.

"Tough luck," sympathized the Lizard. "You sure are the Calamity Kid. But don't worry, we'll land you something else. And remember that that partnership proposition is still open."

There ensued another month of idleness, during which Jimmy again had recourse to the Help Wanted column. The Lizard tried during the first week to find something for him, and then occurred a certain very famous safe-robbery, and the Lizard disappeared.

Part Three

15

LITTLE EVA

EARLY in March Jimmy was again forced to part with his watch. As he was coming out of the pawnshop late in the afternoon he almost collided with Little Eva.

"For the love of Mike!" cried that young lady, "where have you been all this time, and what's happened to you? You look as though you'd lost your last friend." And then noting the shop from which he had emerged and the deduction being all too obvious, she laid one of her shapely hands upon the sleeve of his cheap, ill-fitting coat. "You're up against it, kid, ain't you?" she asked.

"Oh, it's nothing," said Jimmy ruefully. "I'm getting used to it."

"I guess you're too square," said the girl. "I heard about that Brophy business." And then she laughed softly. "Do you know who the biggest backers of that graft were?"

"No," said Jimmy.

"Well, don't laugh yourself to death," she admonished. "They were Steve Murray and Feinheimer. Talk about sore pups! You never saw anything like it, and when they found who it was that had ditched their wonderful scheme they threw another fit. Say, those birds have been weeping on each other's shoulders ever since."

"Do you still breakfast at Feinheimer's?" asked Jimmy.

"Once in a while," said the girl, "but not so often now." And she dropped her eyes to the ground in what, in another than Little Eva, might have been construed as embarrassment. "Where you going now?" she asked quickly.

"To eat," said Jimmy, and then prompted by the instincts of his earlier training and with appreciable pause: "Won't you take dinner with me?"

"No," said the girl, "but you are going to take dinner with me. You're out of a job and broke, and the chances are you've just this minute hocked your watch, while I have plenty of money. No," she said as Jimmy started to protest, "this is going to be on me. I never knew how much I enjoyed talking with you at breakfast until after you had left Feinheimer's. I've been real lonesome ever since," she admitted frankly. "You talk to me different from what the other men do." She pressed his arm gently. "You talk to me, kid, just like a fellow might talk to his sister."

Jimmy didn't know just what rejoinder to make, and so he made none. As a matter of fact, he had not realized that he had said or done anything to win her confidence, nor could he explain his attitude toward her in the light of what he knew of her life and vocation. There is a type of man that respects and reveres womanhood for those inherent virtues which are supposed to be the natural attributes of the sex because in their childhood they have seen them exemplified in their mothers, their sisters and in the majority of women and girls who were parts of the natural environment of their early lives.

It is difficult ever entirely to shatter the faith of such men, and however they may be wronged by individuals of the opposite sex their subjective attitude toward woman in the abstract is one of chivalrous respects. As far as outward appearances were concerned Little Eva might have passed readily as a paragon of all the virtues. As yet, there was no sign nor line of dissipation marked upon her piquant face, nor in her consociation with Jimmy was there ever the slightest reference to or reminder of her vocation.

They chose a quiet and eminently respectable dining place, and after they had ordered, Jimmy spread upon the table an evening paper he had purchased upon the street.

"Help me find a job," he said to the girl, and together the two ran through the want columns.

"Here's a bunch of them," cried the girl laughingly, "all in one ad. Night cook, one hundred and fifty dollars; swing man, one hundred and forty dollars; roast cook, one hundred and twenty dollars; broiler, one hundred and twenty dollars. I'd better apply for that. Fry cook, one hundred and ten dollars. Oh, here's something for Steve Murray: chicken butcher, eighty dollars; here's a job I'd like," she cried, "ice-cream man, one hundred dollars."

"Quit your kidding," said Jimmy. "I'm looking for a job, not an acrostic."

"Well," she said, "here are two solid pages of them, but nobody seems to want a waiter. What else can you do?" she asked, smiling up at him.

"I can drive a milk-wagon," said Jimmy, "but the drivers are all on strike."

"Now, be serious," she announced. "Let's look for something really good. Here's somebody wants a finishing superintendent for a string music instrument factory, and a business manager and electrical engineer in this one. What's an efficiency expert?"

"Oh, he's a fellow who gums up the works, puts you three weeks behind in less than a week and has all your best men resigning inside of a month. I know, because my dad had one at his plant a few years ago."

The girl looked at him for a moment. "Your father is a business man?" she asked, and without waiting for an answer. "Why don't you work for him?"

It was the first reference that Jimmy had ever made to his connections or his past.

"Oh," he said, "he's a long way off and—if I'm no good to any one here I certainly wouldn't be any good to him."

His companion made no comment, but resumed her reading of the advertisement before her:

> WANTED, an Efficiency Expert—Machine works wants man capable of thoroughly reorganizing large business along modern lines, stopping leaks and systematizing every activity.

Call International Machine Company, West Superior Street. Ask for Mr. Compton.

"What do you have to know to be an efficiency expert?" asked the girl.

"From what I saw of the bird I just mentioned the less one knows about anything the more successful he should be as an efficiency expert, for he certainly didn't know anything. And yet the results from kicking everybody in the plant out of his own particular rut eventually worked wonders for the organization. If the man had had any sense, tact or diplomacy nothing would have been accomplished."

"Why don't you try it?" asked the girl. Jimmy looked at her with a quizzical smile. "Thank you," he said.

"Oh, I didn't mean it that way," she cried. "But from what you tell me I imagine that all a man needs is a front and plenty of punch. You've got the front all right with your looks and gift of gab, and I leave it to Young Brophy if you haven't got the punch."

"Maybe that's not the punch an efficiency expert needs," suggested Jimmy.

"It might be a good thing to have up his sleeve," replied the girl, and then suddenly, "do you believe in hunches?"

"Sometimes," replied Jimmy.

"Well, this is a hunch, take it from me," she continued. "I'll bet you can land that job and make good."

"What makes you think so?" asked Jimmy.

"I don't know," she replied, "but you know what a woman's intuition is."

"I suppose," said Jimmy, "that it's the feminine of hunch. But however good your hunch or intuition may be it would certainly get a terrible jolt if I presented myself to the head of the International Machine Company in this scenery. Do you see anything about my clothes that indicates efficiency?"

"It isn't your clothes that count, Jimmy," she said, "it's the combination of that face of yours and what you've got in your head. You're the most efficient looking person I ever saw, and if you want a reference I'll say this much for you, you're the most efficient waiter that Feinheimer ever had. He said so himself, even after he canned you."

"Your enthusiasm," said Jimmy, "is contagious. If it wasn't for these sorry rags of mine I'd take a chance on that hunch of yours."

The girl laid her hand impulsively upon his.

"Won't you let me help you?" she asked. "I'd like to, and it will only be a loan if you wanted to look at it that way. Enough to get you a decent-looking outfit, such an outfit as you ought to have to land a good job. I know, and everybody else knows, that clothes do count no matter what we say to the contrary. I'll bet you're some looker when you're dolled up! Please," she continued, "won't you please, just try it for a gamble?"

"I don't see how I can," he objected. "The chances are I could never pay you back, and there is no reason in the world why you should loan me money. You are certainly under no obligation to me."

"I wish you would let me, Jimmy," she said. "It would make me awfully happy!"

The man hesitated.

"Oh," she said, "I'm going to do it, anyway. Wait a minute," and, rising, she left the table.

In a few minutes she returned. "Here," she said, "you've got to take it," and extended her hand toward him beneath the edge of the table.

"I can't," said Jimmy. "It wouldn't be right."

The girl looked at him and flushed.

"Do you mean," she said, "because it's my—because of what I am?"

"Oh, no," said Jimmy; "please don't think that!" And impulsively he took her hand beneath the table. At the contact the girl caught her breath with a little quick-drawn sigh.

"Here, take it!" she said, and drawing her hand away quickly, left a roll of bills in Jimmy's hand.

16

JIMMY THROWS A BLUFF

THAT afternoon Mr. Harold Bince had entered his superior's office with an afternoon paper in his hand.

"What's the idea of this ad, Mr. Compton?" he asked. "Why do we need an efficiency expert? I wish you had let me know what you intended doing."

"I knew that if I told you, Harold, you would object," said the older man, "and I thought I would have a talk with several applicants before saying anything about it to any one. Of course, whoever we get will work with you, but I would rather not have it generally known about the plant. There seems to be a leak somewhere and evidently we are too close to the work to see it ourselves. It will require an outsider to discover it."

"I am very much opposed to the idea," said Bince. "These fellows usually do nothing more than disrupt an organization. We have a force that has been here, many of them, for years. There is as little lost motion in this plant as in any in the country, and if we start in saddling these men with a lot of red-tape which will necessitate their filling out innumerable forms for every job, about half their time will be spent in bookkeeping, which can just as well be done here in the office as it is now. I hope that you will reconsider your intention and let us work out our own solution in a practical manner, which we can do better in the light of our own experience than can an outsider who knows nothing of our peculiar problems."

"We will not permit the organization to be disrupted," replied Mr. Compton. "It may do a lot of good to get a new angle on our problems and at least it will do no harm."

"I can't agree with you," replied Bince. "I think it will do a lot of harm."

Compton looked at his watch. "It is getting late, Harold," he said, "and this is pay-day. I should think Everitt could help you with the pay-roll." Everitt was the cashier.

"I prefer to do it myself," replied Bince. "Everitt has about all he can do, and anyway, I don't like to trust it to any one else." And realizing that Compton did not care to discuss the matter of the efficiency expert further Bince returned to his own office.

The following afternoon the office boy entered Mr. Compton's office. "A gentleman to see you, sir," he announced. "He said to tell you that he came in reply to your advertisement."

"Show him in," instructed Compton, and a moment later Jimmy entered—a rehabilitated Jimmy. Upon his excellent figure the ready-made suit had all the appearance of faultlessly tailored garments. Compton looked up at his visitor, and with the glance he swiftly appraised Jimmy—a glance that assured him that here might be just the man he wanted, for intelligence, aggressiveness and efficiency were evidently the outstanding characteristics of the young man before him. After Jimmy had presented himself the other motioned him to a chair.

"I am looking," said Mr. Compton, "for an experienced man who can come in here and find out just what is wrong with us. We have an old-established business which has been making money for years. We are taking all the work that we can possibly handle at the highest prices we have ever received, and yet our profits are not at all commensurate with the volume of business. It has occurred to me that an experienced man from the outside would be able to more quickly put his finger on the leaks and stop them. Now tell me just what your experience has been and we will see if we can come to some understanding."

From his pocket Jimmy drew a half-dozen envelopes, and taking the contents from them one by one laid them on the desk before Mr. Compton. On the letterheads of half a dozen large out-of-town manufacturers in various lines were brief but eulogistic comments upon the work done in their plants by Mr. James Torrance, Jr. As he was reading them Mr. Compton glanced up by chance to see that the face of the applicant was slightly flushed, which he thought undoubtedly due to the fact that the other knew he was reading the words of praise contained in the letters, whereas the truth of the matter was that Jimmy's color was heightened by a feeling of guilt.

"These are very good," said Mr. Compton, looking up from the letters. "I don't know that I need go any further. A great deal depends on a man's personality in a position of this sort, and from your appearance I should imagine that you're all right along that line and you seem to have had the right kind of experience. Now, what arrangement can we make?"

Jimmy had given the matter of pay considerable thought, but the trouble was that he did not know what an efficiency expert might be expected to demand. He recalled vaguely that the one his father had employed got something like ten dollars a day, or one hundred a day, Jimmy couldn't remember which, and so he was afraid that he might ask too much and lose the opportunity, or too little and reveal that he had no knowledge of the value of such services.

"I would rather leave that to you," he said. "What do you think the work would be worth to you?"

"Do you expect to continue in this line of work?" asked Mr. Compton. "When the job is finished you would want to go somewhere else, I suppose?"

Jimmy saw an opening and leaped for it. "Oh, no!" he replied. "On the contrary, I wouldn't mind working into a permanent position, and if you think there might be a possibility of that I would consider a reasonable salary arrangement rather than the usual contract rate for expert service."

"It is very possible," said Mr. Compton, "that if you are the right man there would be a permanent place in the organization for you. With that idea in mind I should say that two hundred and fifty dollars a month might be a mutually fair arrangement to begin with."

Two hundred and fifty dollars a month! Jimmy tried to look bored, but not too bored.

"Of course," he said, "with the idea that it may become a permanent, well-paying position I think I might be inclined to consider it—in fact, I am very favorably inclined toward it," he added hastily as he thought he noted a sudden waning of interest in Compton's expression. "But be sure yourself that I am the man you want. For instance, my methods—you should know something of them first."

In Jimmy's pocket was a small book he had purchased at a second-hand bookshop the evening before, upon the cover of which appeared the title "How to Get More Out of Your Factory." He had not had sufficient time to study it thoroughly, but had succeeded in memorizing several principal headings on the contents page.

"At first," he explained, "I won't seem to be accomplishing much, as I always lay the foundation of my future work by studying my men. Some men have that within them which spurs them on; while some need artificial initiative—outside encouragement," he quoted glibly from "How to Get More Out of Your Factory." "Some men extend themselves under stern discipline; some respond only to a gentle rein. I study men—the men over me, under me, around me. I study them and learn how to get from each the most that is in him. At the same time I shall be looking for leaks and investigating time-keeping methods, wage-paying systems and planning on efficiency producers. Later I shall start reducing costs by studying machines, handling material economically and producing power at lowest cost; keeping the product moving, making environment count on the balance-sheet and protecting against accident and fire." This was as far as Jimmy had memorized, and so he stopped.

"I think," said Mr. Compton, "that you have the right idea. Some of your points are not entirely clear to me, as there are many modern methods that I have not, I am sorry to say, investigated sufficiently."

Jimmy did not think it necessary to explain that they were not clear to him either.

"And now," said Compton, "if you are satisfied with the salary, when can you start?"

Jimmy rose with a brisk and businesslike manner. "I am free now," he said, "with the exception of a little personal business which I can doubtless finish up to-morrow—suppose I come Thursday?"

"Good," exclaimed Compton, "but before you go I want you to meet our assistant general manager, Mr. Bince." And he led Jimmy toward Bince's office.

"This is Mr. Torrance, Harold," said Mr. Compton as they entered, "Mr. Bince, Mr. Torrance. Mr. Torrance is going to help us systematize the plant. He will report directly to me and I know you will do everything in your power to help him. You can go to Mr. Bince for anything in the way of information you require, and Harold, when Mr. Torrance comes Thursday I wish you would introduce him to Everitt and the various department heads and explain that they are to give him full cooperation. And now, as I have an appointment, I shall have to ask you to excuse me. I will see you Thursday. If there are any questions you want to ask, Mr. Bince will be glad to give you any information you wish or care for."

Jimmy had felt from the moment that he was introduced to Bince that the latter was antagonistic and now that the two were alone together he was not long left in doubt as to the correctness of his surmise. As soon as the door had closed behind Mr. Compton Bince wheeled toward Jimmy.

"I don't mind telling you, Mr. Torrance," he said, "that I consider the services of an expert absolutely unnecessary, but if Mr. Compton wishes to experiment I will interfere in no way and I shall help you all I can, but I sincerely hope that you, on your part, will refrain from interfering with my activities. As a matter of fact, you won't have to leave this office to get all the information you need, and if you will come to me I can make it easy for you to investigate the entire workings of the plant and save you a great deal of unnecessary personal labor. I suppose that you have had a great deal of experience along this line?"

Jimmy nodded affirmatively.

"Just how do you purpose proceeding?"

"Oh, well," said Jimmy, "each one of us really

has a system of his own. At first I won't seem to be accomplishing much, as I always lay the foundation of my future work by studying my men. Some men have that within them which spurs them on; while some need artificial initiative—outside encouragement." He hoped that the door to Compton's office was securely closed.

"Some men extend themselves under stern discipline; some respond only to a gentle rein. I study men—the men over me, under me, around me. I study them and learn how to get from each the most that is in him. At the same time I shall be looking for leaks and investigating time-keeping methods"—he was looking straight at Bince and he could not help but note the slight narrowing of the other's lids—"wage-paying systems and planning on efficiency producers."

Here he hesitated a moment as though weighing his words, though as a matter of fact he had merely forgotten the title of the next chapter, but presently he went on again:

"Later I shall start reducing costs by studying machines, handling material economically and producing power at lowest costs; keeping the product moving, making environment count on the balance-sheet and protecting against accident and fire."

"Is that all?" asked Mr. Bince.

"Oh, no, indeed!" said Jimmy. "That's just a very brief outline of the way I shall start."

"Ah!" said Mr. Bince. "And just how, may I ask, do you make environment count on the balance-sheet? I do not quite understand."

Jimmy was mentally gasping and going down for the third time. He had wondered when he read that chapter title just what it might mean.

"Oh," he said, "you will understand that thoroughly when we reach that point. It is one of the steps in my method. Other things lead up to it. It is really rather difficult to explain until we have a concrete example, something that you can really visualize, you know. But I assure you that it will be perfectly plain to you when we arrive at that point.

"And now," he said, rising, "I must be going. I have a great deal to attend to this afternoon and tomorrow, as I wish to get some personal matters out of the way before I start in here Thursday."

"All right," said Mr. Bince, "I suppose we shall see you Thursday, but just bear in mind, please, that you and I can work better together than at cross-purposes."

17

JIMMY ON THE JOB

AS Jimmy left the office he discovered that those last words of Bince's had made a considerable and a rather unfavorable impression on him. He was sure that there was an underlying meaning, though just what it portended he was unable to imagine.

From the International Machine Company Jimmy went directly to the restaurant where he and Little Eva had dined the night before. He found her waiting for him, as they had agreed she would.

"Well, what luck?" she asked as he took the chair next to her.

"Oh, I landed the job all right," said Jimmy, "but I feel like a crook. I don't know how in the world I ever came to stand for those letters of recommendation. They were the things that got me the job all right, but I honestly feel just as though I had stolen something."

"Don't feel that way," said the girl. "You'll make good, I know, and then it won't make any difference about the letters."

"And now," said Jimmy, "tell me where you got

them. You promised me that you would tell me afterward."

"Oh," said the girl, "that was easy. A girl who rooms at the same place I do works in a big printing and engraving plant and I got her to get me some samples of letter-heads early this morning. In fact, I went down-town with her when she went to work, and then I went over to the Underwood offices and wrote the recommendations out on a machine—I used to be a stenographer."

"And you forged these names?" asked Jimmy, horrified.

"I didn't forge anybody's name," replied the girl. "I made them up."

"You mean there are no such men?"

"As far as I know there are not," she replied, laughing.

Slowly Jimmy drew the letters from his inside pocket and read them one by one, spreading them out upon the table before him. Presently he looked up at the girl.

"Why don't you get a position again as a stenographer?" he asked.

"I have been thinking of it," she said; "do you want me to?"

"Yes," he said, "I want you to very much."

"It will be easy," she said. "There is no reason why I shouldn't except that there was no one ever cared what I did."

As she finished speaking they were both aware that a man had approached their table and stopped opposite them. Jimmy and the girl looked up to see a large man in a dark suit looking down at Eva.

Jimmy did not recognize the man, but he knew at once what he was.

"Well, O'Donnell, what's doing?" asked the girl.

"You know what's doing," said the officer. "How miny toimes do the capt'in have to be afther isshuin' orrders tellin' you janes to kape out uv dacent places?"

The girl flushed. "I'm not working here," she said.

"Tu hell ye ain't," sneered O'Donnell. "Didn't I see ye flag this guy whin he came in?"

"This young lady is a friend of mine," said Jimmy. "I had an appointment to meet her here."

O'Donnell shifted his gaze from the girl to her escort and for the first time appraised Jimmy thoroughly. "Oh, it's you, is it?" he asked.

"It is," said Jimmy; "you guessed it the first time, but far be it from me to know what you have guessed, as I never saw you before, my friend."

"Well, I've seen you before," said O'Donnell, "and ye put one over on me that time all roight, I can see now. I don't know what your game was, but you and the Lizard played it pretty slick when you could pull the wool over Patrick O'Donnell's eyes the way ye done."

"Oh," said Jimmy, "I've got you now. You're the bull who interfered with my friend and me on Randolph and La Salle 'way back last July."

"I am," said O'Donnell, "and I thought ye was a foine young gentleman, and you are a foine one," he said with intense sarcasm.

"Go away and leave us alone," said the girl. "We're not doing anything. We ate in here last night together. This man is perfectly respectable. He isn't what you think him, at all."

"I'm not going to pinch him," said O'Donnell; "I ain't got nothin' to pinch him for, but the next time I see him I'll know him."

"Well," said the girl, "are you going to beat it or are you going to stick around here bothering us all evening? There hasn't anybody registered a complaint against me in here."

"Naw," said O'Donnell, "they ain't, but you want to watch your step or they will."

"All right," said the girl, "run along and sell your papers." And she turned again to Jimmy, and as though utterly unconscious of the presence of the police officer, she remarked, "That big stiff gives me a pain. He's the original Buttinsky Kid."

O'Donnell flushed. "Watch your step, young lady," he said as he turned and walked away.

"I thought," said Jimmy, "that it was the customary practise to attempt to mollify the guardians of the law."

"Mollify nothing," returned the girl. "None of these big bruisers knows what decency is, and if you're decent to them they think you're afraid of them. When they got something on you you got to be nice, but when they haven't, tell them where they get off. I knew he wouldn't pinch me; he's got nothing to pinch me for, and he'd have been out of luck if he had, for there hasn't one of them got anything on me."

"But won't he have it in for you?" asked Jimmy.

"Sure, he will," said the girl. "He's got it in for everybody. That's what being a policeman does to a man. Say, most of these guys hate themselves. I tell you, though," she said presently and more seriously, "I'm sorry on your account. These dicks never forget a face. He's got you catalogued and filed away in what he calls his brain alongside of a dip and—a"—she hesitated—"a girl like me, and no matter how high up you ever get if your foot slips up will bob O'Donnell with these two facts."

"I'm not worrying," said Jimmy. "I don't intend to let my foot slip in his direction."

"I hope not," said the girl.

Thursday morning Jimmy took up his duties as efficiency expert at the plant of the International Machine Company. Since his interview with Compton his constant companion had been "How to Get More Out of Your Factory," with the result that he felt that unless he happened to be pitted against another efficiency expert he could at least make a noise like efficiency, and also he had grasped what he considered the fundamental principle of efficiency, namely, simplicity.

"If," he reasoned, "I cannot find in any plant hundreds of operations that are not being done in the simplest manner it will be because I haven't even ordinary powers of observation or intelligence," for after his second interview with Compton, Jimmy had suddenly realized that the job meant something to him beside the two hundred and fifty dollars a month—that he couldn't deliberately rob Compton, as he felt that he would be doing unless he could give value received in services, and he meant to do his best to accomplish that end.

He knew that for a while his greatest asset would be bluff, but there was something about Mason Compton that had inspired in the young man a vast respect and another sentiment that he realized upon better acquaintance might ripen into affection. Compton reminded him in many ways of his father, and with the realization of that resemblance Jimmy felt more and more ashamed of the part he was playing, but now that he had gone into it he made up his mind that he would stick to it, and there was besides the slight encouragement that he had derived from the enthusiasm of the girl who had suggested the idea to him and of her oft-repeated assertion relative to her "hunch" that he would make good.

18

THE EFFICIENCY EXPERT

UNLIKE most other plants the International Machine Company paid on Monday, and it was on the Monday following his assumption of his new duties that Jimmy had his first clash with Bince. He had been talking with Everitt, the cashier, whom, in accordance with his "method," he was studying. From Everitt he had learned that it was pay-day and he had asked the cashier to let him see the pay-roll.

"I don't handle the pay-roll," replied Everitt a trifle peevishly. "Shortly after Mr. Bince was made assistant general manager a new rule was promulgated, to the effect that all salaries and wages were to be considered as confidential and that no one but the assistant general manager would handle the pay-rolls. All I know is the amount of the weekly check. He hires and fires everybody and pays everybody."

"Rather unusual, isn't it?" commented Jimmy.

"Very," said Everitt. "Here's some of us have been with Mr. Compton since Bince was in long clothes, and then he comes in here and says that we are not to be trusted with the pay-roll."

"Well," said Jimmy, "I shall have to go to him to see it then."

"He won't show it to you," said Everitt.

"Oh, I guess he will," said Jimmy, and a moment later he knocked at Bince's office door. When Bince saw who it was he turned back to his work with a grunt.

"I am sorry, Torrance," he said, "but I can't talk with you just now. I'm very busy."

"Working on the pay-roll?" said Jimmy.

"Yes," snarled Bince.

"That's what I came in to see," said the efficiency expert.

"Impossible," said Bince. "The International Machine Company's pay-roll is confidential, absolutely confidential. Nobody sees it but me or Mr. Compton if he wishes to."

"I understood from Mr. Compton," said Jimmy, "that I was to have full access to all records."

"That merely applied to operation records," said Bince. "It had nothing to do with the pay-roll."

"I should consider the pay-roll very closely allied to operations," responded Jimmy.

"I shouldn't," said Bince.

"You won't let me see it then?" demanded Jimmy.

"Look here," said Bince, "we agreed that we wouldn't interfere with each other. I haven't interfered with you. Now don't you interfere with me. This is my work, and my office is not being investigated by any efficiency expert or any one else."

"I don't recall that I made any such agreement," said Jimmy. "I must insist on seeing that pay-roll."

Bince turned white with suppressed anger, and then suddenly slamming his pen on the desk, he wheeled around toward the other.

"I might as well tell you something," he said, "that will make your path easier here, if you know it. I understand that you want a permanent job with us. If you do you might as well understand now as any other time that you have got to be satisfactory to me. Of course, it is none of your business, but it may help you to understand conditions when I tell you that I am to marry Mr. Compton's daugher, and when I do that he expects to retire from business, leaving me in full charge here. Now, do you get me?"

Jimmy had involuntarily acquired antipathy toward Bince at their first meeting, an antipathy which had been growing the more that he saw of the assistant general manager. This fact, coupled with Bince's present rather nasty manner, was rapidly arousing the anger of the efficiency expert.

"I didn't come in here," he said, "to discuss your matrimonial prospects, Mr. Bince. I came in here to see the pay-roll, and you will oblige me by letting me see it."

"I tell you again," said Bince, "once and for all, that you don't see the pay-roll nor anything else connected with my office, and you will oblige me by not bothering me any longer. As I told you when you first came in, I am very busy."

Jimmy turned and left the room. He was on the point of going to Compton's office and asking for authority to see the pay-roll, and then it occurred to him that Compton would probably not take sides against his assistant general manager and future son-in-law.

"I've got to get at it some other way," said Jimmy, "but you bet your life I'm going to get at it. It looks to me as though there's something funny about that pay-roll."

On his way out he stopped at Everitt's cage. "What was the amount of the check for the pay-roll for this week, Everitt?" he asked.

"A little over ninety-six hundred dollars."

"Thanks," said Jimmy, and returned to the shops to continue his study of his men, and as he studied them he asked many questions, made many notes in his little note-book, and always there were two questions that were the same: "What is your name? What wages do you get?"

"I guess," said Jimmy, "that in a short time I will know as much about the pay-roll as the assistant general manager."

Nor was it the pay-roll only that claimed Jimmy's attention. He found that several handlings of materials could be eliminated by the adoption of simple changes, and that a rearrangement of some of the machines removed the necessity for long hauls from one part of the shop to another. After an evening with the little volume he had purchased for twenty-five cents in the second-hand bookshop he ordered changes that enabled him to cut five men from the pay-roll and at the same time do the work more expeditiously and efficiently.

"Little book," he said one evening, "I take my hat off to you. You are the best two-bits' worth I ever purchased."

The day following the completion of the changes he had made in the shop he was in Compton's office.

"Patton was explaining some of the changes you have made," remarked Compton. Patton was the shop foreman. "He said they were so simple that he wondered none of us had thought of them before. I quite agree with him."

"So do I," returned Jimmy, "but, then, my whole method is based upon simplicity." And his mind traveled to the unpretentious little book on the table in his room on Indiana Avenue.

"The feature that appeals to me most strongly is that you have been able to get the cooperation of the men," continued Compton; "that's what I feared—that they wouldn't accept your suggestions. How did you do it?"

"I showed them how they could turn out more work and make more money by my plan. This appealed to the piece-workers. I demonstrated to the others that the right way is the easiest way—I showed them how they could earn their wages with less effort."

"Good," said Compton. "You are running into no difficulties then? Is there any way in which I can help you?"

"I am getting the best kind of cooperation from

the men in the shop, practically without exception," replied Jimmy, "although there is one fellow, a straw boss named Krovac, who does not seem to take as kindly to the changes I have made as the others, but he really doesn't amount to anything as an obstacle." Jimmy also thought of Bince and the pay-roll, but he was still afraid to broach the subject. Suddenly an inspiration came to him.

"Yes," he said, "I believe your accounting system could be improved—it will take me months to get around to it, as my work is primarily in the shop, at first, at least. You can save both time and money by having your books audited by a firm of public accountants who can also suggest a new and more up-to-date system."

"Not a bad idea," said Compton. "I think we will do it."

For another half-hour they discussed Jimmy's work, and then as the latter was leaving Compton stopped him.

"By the way, you don't happen to know of a good stenographer, do you? Miss Withe is leaving me Saturday."

Jimmy thought a moment. Instantly he thought of Little Eva and what she had said of her experience as a stenographer, and her desire to abandon her present life for something in the line of her former work. Here was a chance to repay her in some measure for her kindness to him.

"Yes," he said, "I do know of a young lady who, I believe, could do the work. Shall I have her call on you?"

"If you will, please," replied Compton.

As Jimmy left the office Compton rang for Bince, and when the latter came, told him of his plan to employ a firm of accountants to renovate their entire system of bookkeeping.

"Is that one of Torrance's suggestions?" asked Bince.

"Yes, the idea is his," replied Compton, "and I think it is a good one."

"It seems to me," said Bince, "that Torrance is balling things up sufficiently as it is without getting in other theorizers who have no practical knowledge of our business. The result of all this will be to greatly increase our overhead by saddling us with a lot of red-tape in the accounting department similar to that which Torrance is loading the producing end with."

"I am afraid that you are prejudiced, Harold," said Compton. "I cannot discover that Torrance is doing anything to in any way complicate the shop work. As a matter of fact, a single change which he has just made has resulted in our performing certain operations in less time and to better advantage with five less men than formerly. Just in this one thing he has not only more than earned his salary, but is really paying dividends on our investment."

Bince was silent for a moment. He had walked to the window and was looking out on the street below, then he turned suddenly toward Compton.

"Mr. Compton," he said, "you have made me assistant general manager here and now, just when I am reaching a point where I feel I can accomplish something, you are practically taking the authority out of my hands and putting it in that of a stranger.

I feel not only that you are making a grave mistake, but that it is casting a reflection on my work. It is making a difference in the attitude of the men toward me that I am afraid can never be overcome, and consequently while lessening my authority it is also lessening my value to the plant. I am going to ask you to drop this whole idea. As assistant general manager, I feel that it is working injury to the organization, and I hope that before it is too late—that, in fact, immediately, you will discharge Torrance and drop this idea of getting outsiders to come in and install a new accounting system."

"You're altogether too sensitive, Harold," replied Compton. "It is no reflection on you whatsoever. The system under which we have been working is, with very few exceptions, the very system that I evolved myself through years of experience in this business. If there is any reflection upon any one it is upon me and not you. You must learn to realize, if you do not already, what I realize—that no one is infallible. Just because the system is mine or yours we must not think that no better system can be devised. I am perfectly satisfied with what Mr. Torrance is doing, and I agree with his suggestion that we employ a firm of accountants, but I think no less of you or your ability on that account."

Bince saw that it was futile to argue the matter further.

"Very well, sir," he said. "I hope that I am mistaken and that no serious harm will result. When do you expect to start these accountants in?"

"Immediately," replied Compton. "I shall get in

touch with somebody to-day."

Bince shook his head dubiously as he returned to his own office.

19

PLOTTING

THE following Monday Miss Edith Hudson went to work for the International Machine Company as Mr. Compton's stenographer. Nor could the most fastidious have discovered aught to criticise in the appearance or deportment of "Little Eva."

The same day the certified public accountants came. Mr. Harold Bince appeared nervous and irritable, and he would have been more nervous and more irritable had he known that Jimmy had just learned the amount of the pay-check from Everitt and that he had discovered that, although five men had been laid off and no new ones employed since the previous week, the payroll check was practically the same as before—approximately one thousand dollars more than his note-book indicated it should be.

"Phew!" whistled Jimmy. "These C.P.A.'s are going to find this a more interesting job than they anticipated. Poor old Compton! I feel mighty sorry for him, but he had better find it out now than after that grafter has wrecked his business entirely."

That afternoon Mr. Compton left the office earlier than usual, complaining of a headache, and the next morning his daughter telephoned that he was ill and would not come to the office that day. During the morning as Bince was walking through the shop he stopped to talk with Krovac.

Pete Krovac was a rat-faced little foreigner, looked upon among the men as a trouble-maker. He nursed a perpetual grievance against his employer and his job, and whenever the opportunity presented, and sometimes when it did not present itself, he endeavored to inoculate others with his dissatisfaction. Bince had hired the man, and during the several months that Krovac had been with the company, the assistant general manager had learned enough from other workers to realize that the man was an agitator and a trouble-maker. Several times he had been upon the point of discharging him, but now he was glad that he had not, for he thought he saw in him a type that in the light of present conditions might be of use to him.

In fact, for the past couple of weeks he had been using the man in an endeavor to get some information concerning Torrance and his methods that would permit him to go to Compton with a valid argument for Jimmy's discharge.

"Well, Krovac," he said as he came upon the man, "is Torrance interfering with you any now?"

"He hasn't got my job yet," growled the other, "but he's letting out hard-working men with families without any reason. The first thing you know you'll have a strike on your hands."

"I haven't heard any one else complaining," said Bince.

"You will, though," replied Krovac. "They don't any of us know when we are going to be canned to give Compton more profit, and men are not going to stand for that long."

"Then," said Bince, "I take it that he really hasn't interfered with you much?"

"Oh, he's always around asking a lot of fool questions," said Krovac. "Last week he asked every man in the place what his name was and what wages he was getting. Wrote it all down in a little book. I suppose he is planning on cutting pay."

Bince's eyes narrowed. "He got that information from every man in the shop?" he asked.

"Yes," replied Krovac.

Bince was very pale. He stood in silence for some minutes, apparently studying the man before him. At last he spoke.

"Krovac," he said, "you don't like this man Torrance, do you?"

"No," said the other, "I don't."

"Neither do I," said Bince. "I know his plans even better than you. This shop has short hours and good pay, but if we don't get rid of him it will have the longest hours and lowest pay of any shop in the city."

"Well?" questioned Krovac.

"I think," said Bince, "that there ought to be some way to prevent this man doing any further harm here."

He looked straight into Krovac's eyes.

"There is," muttered the latter.

"It would be worth something of course," suggested Bince.

"How much?" asked Krovac.

"Oh, I should think it ought to be worth a hundred dollars." replied Bince.

Krovac thought for a moment.

"I think I can arrange it," he said, "but I would have to have fifty now."

"I cannot give it to you here," said Bince, "but if I should happen to pass through the shop this afternoon you might find an envelope on the floor beside your machine after I have gone."

The following evening as Jimmy alighted from the Indiana Avenue car at Eighteenth Street, two men left the car behind him. He did not notice them, although, as he made his way toward his boarding-house, he heard footsteps directly in his rear, and suddenly noting that they were approaching him rapidly, he involuntarily cast a glance behind him just as one of the men raised an arm to strike at him with what appeared to be a short piece of pipe.

Jimmy dodged the blow and then both men sprang for him. The first one Jimmy caught on the point of the chin with a blow that put its recipient out of the fight before he got into it, and then his companion, who was the larger, succeeded in closing with the efficiency expert. Inadvertently, however, he caught Jimmy about the neck, leaving both his intended victim's arms free with the result that the latter was able to seize his antagonist low down about the body, and then pressing him close to him and hurling himself suddenly forward, he threw the fellow backward upon the cement sidewalk with his own body on top. With a resounding whack the attacker's head came in contact with the concrete, his arms relaxed their hold upon Jimmy's neck, and as the latter arose he saw both his assailants, temporarily at least, out of the fighting.

Jimmy glanced hastily in both directions. There was no one in sight. His boarding-house was but a few steps away, and two minutes later he was safe in his room.

"A year ago," he thought to himself, smiling, "my first thought would have been to have called in the police, but the Lizard has evidently given me a new view-point in regard to them," for the latter had impressed upon Jimmy the fact that whatever knowledge a policeman might have regarding one was always acquired with the idea that eventually it might be used against the person to whom it pertained.

"What a policeman don't know about you will never hurt you," was one way that the Lizard put it.

When Jimmy appeared in the shop the next morning he noted casually that Krovac had a cut upon his chin, but he did not give the matter a second thought. Bince had arrived late. His first question, as he entered the small outer office where Mr. Compton's stenographer and his worked, was addressed to Miss Edith Hudson.

"Is Mr. Torrance down yet?" he asked.

"Yes," replied the girl, "he has been here some time. Do you wish to see him?"

Edith thought that the "No" which he snapped at her was a trifle more emphatic than the circumstances seemed to warrant, nor could she help but notice after he had entered his office the vehement manner in which he slammed the door.

"I wonder what's eating him," thought Miss Hudson to herself. "Of course he doesn't like Jimmy, but why is he so peeved because Jimmy came to work this morning—I don't quite get it."

Almost immediately Bince sent for Krovac, and when the latter came and stood before his desk the assistant general manager looked up at him questioningly.

"Well?" he asked.

"Look at my chin," was Krovac's reply, "and he damn near killed the other guy."

"Maybe you'll have better luck the next time," growled Bince.

"There ain't goin' to be no next time," asserted Krovac. "I don't tackle that guy again."

Bince held out his hand.

"All right," he said, "you might return the fifty then."

"Return nothin'," growled Krovac. "I sure done fifty dollars' worth last night."

"Come on," said Bince, "hand over the fifty."

"Nothin' doin'," said Krovac with an angry snarl. "It might be worth another fifty to you to know that I wasn't going to tell old man Compton."

"You damn scoundrel!" exclaimed Bince.

"Don't go callin' me names," admonished Krovac. "A fellow that hires another to croak a man for him for one hundred bucks ain't got no license to call nobody names."

Bince realized only too well that he was absolutely in the power of the fellow and immediately his manner changed.

"Come," he said, "Krovac, there is no use in our quarreling. You can help me and I can help you. There must be some other way to get around this."

"What are you trying to do?" asked Krovac. "I got enough on you now to send you up, and I don't mind tellin' yuh," he added, "that I had a guy hid down there in the shop where he could watch you drop the envelope behind my machine. I got a witness, yuh understand!"

Mr. Bince did understand, but still he managed to control his temper.

"What of it?" he said. "Nobody would believe your story, but let's forget that. What we want to do is get rid of Torrance."

"That isn't all you want to do," said Krovac. "There is something else."

Bince realized that he was compromised as hopelessly already as he could be if the man had even more information.

"Yes," he said, "there is something beside Torrance's interference in the shop. He's interfering with our accounting system and I don't want it interfered with just now."

"You mean the pay-roll?" asked Krovac.

"It might be," said Bince.

"You want them two new guys that are working in the office croaked, too?" asked Krovac.

"I don't want anybody 'croaked,'" replied Bince. "I didn't tell you to kill Torrance in the first place. I just said I didn't want him to come back here to work."

"Ah, hell, what you givin' us?" growled the other. "I knew what you meant and you knew what you meant, too. Come across straight. What do you want?"

"I want all the records of the certified public accountants who are working here," said Bince after a moment's pause. "I want them destroyed, together with the pay-roll records."

"They will all be in the safe in Mr. Compton's office."

Krovac knitted his brows in thought for several moments. "Say," he said, "we can do the whole thing with one job."

"What do you mean?" asked Bince.

"We can get rid of this Torrance guy and get the records, too."

"How?" asked Bince.

"Do you know where Feinheimer's is?"

"Yes."

"Well, you be over there to-night about ten thirty and I'll introduce you to a guy who can pull off this whole thing, and you and I won't have to be mixed up in it at all."

"To-night at ten thirty," said Bince.

"At Feinheimer's," said Krovac.

20

AN INVITATION TO DINE

AS the workman passed through the little outer office Edith Hudson glanced up at him.

"Where," she thought after he had gone, "have I seen that fellow before?"

Jimmy was in the shop applying "How to Get More Out of Your Factory" to the problems of the International Machine Company when he was called to the telephone.

"Is this Mr. Torrance?" asked a feminine voice.

"It is," replied Jimmy.

"I am Miss Compton. My father will probably not be able to get to the office for several days, and as he wishes very much to talk with you he has asked me to suggest that you take dinner with us this evening."

"Thank you," said Jimmy. "Tell Mr. Compton that I will come to the house right after the shop closes to-night."

"I suppose," said Elizabeth Compton as she turned away from the phone, "that an efficiency expert is a very superior party and that his conversation will be far above my head."

Compton laughed. "Torrance seems to be a very likable chap," he said, "and as far as his work is concerned he is doing splendidly."

"Harold doesn't think so," said Elizabeth. "He is terribly put out about the fellow. He told me only the other night that he really believed that it would take years to overcome the bad effect that this man has had upon the organization and upon the work in general."

"That is all poppycock," exclaimed Compton, rather more irritably than was usual with him. "For some reason Harold has taken an unwarranted dislike to this man, but I am watching him closely, and I will see that no very serious mistakes are made."

When Jimmy arrived at the Compton home he was ushered into the library where Mr. Compton was sitting. In a corner of the room, with her back toward the door, Elizabeth Compton sat reading. She did not lay aside her book or look in his direction as Jimmy entered, for the man was in no sense a guest in the light of her understanding of the term. He was merely one of her father's employees here on business to see him, doubtless a very ordinary sort of person whom she would, of course, have to meet when dinner was announced, but not one for whom it was necessary to put oneself out in any way.

Mr. Compton rose and greeted Jimmy cordially and then turned toward his daughter.

"Elizabeth," he said, "this is Mr. Torrance, the efficiency expert at the plant."

Leisurely Miss Compton laid aside her book. Rising, she faced the newcomer, and as their eyes met, Jimmy barely stifled a gasp of astonishment and dismay. Elizabeth Compton's arched brows raised slightly and involuntarily she breathed a low ejaculation, "Efficiency expert!"

Simultaneously there flashed through the minds of both in rapid succession a series of recollections of their previous meetings. The girl saw the clerk at the stocking-counter, the waiter at Feinheimer's, the prize-fighter at the training quarters and the milk-wagon driver. All these things passed through her mind in the brief instant of the introduction and her acknowledgment of it. She was too well-bred to permit any outward indication of her recognition of the man other than the first almost inaudible ejaculation that had been surprised from her.

The indifference she had felt prior to meeting the efficiency expert was altered now to a feeling of keen interest as she realized that she held the power to relieve Bince of the further embarrassment of the man's activities in the plant, and also to save her father from the annoyance and losses that Bince had assured her would result from Torrance's methods. And so she greeted Jimmy Torrance pleasantly, almost cordially.

"I am delighted," she said, "but I am afraid that I am a little awed, too, as I was just saying to father before you came that I felt an efficiency expert must be a very superior sort of person."

If she placed special emphasis on the word "superior" it was so cleverly done that it escaped the notice of her father.

"Oh, not at all," replied Jimmy. "We efficiency experts are really quite ordinary people. One is apt to meet us in any place that nice people are supposed to go."

Elizabeth felt the color rising slowly to her cheek. She realized then that if she had thrown down the gage of battle the young man had lost no time in taking it up.

"I am afraid," she said, "that I do not understand very much about the nature or the purpose of your work, but I presume the idea is to make the concern with which you are connected more prosperous—more successful?"

"Yes," said her father, "that is the idea, and even in the short time he has been with us Mr. Torrance has effected some very excellent changes."

"It must be very interesting work," commented the girl; "a profession that requires years of particular experience and study, and I suppose one must be really thoroughly efficient and successful himself, too, before he can help to improve upon the methods of others or to bring them greater prosperity."

"Quite true," said Jimmy. "Whatever a man undertakes he should succeed in before he can hope to bring success to others."

"Even in trifling occupations, I presume," suggested the girl, "efficiency methods are best—an efficiency expert could doubtlessly drive a milk-wagon better than an ordinary person?" And she looked straight into Jimmy's eyes, an unquestioned challenge in her own.

"Unquestionably," said Jimmy. "He could wait on table better, too."

"Or sell stockings?" suggested Elizabeth.

It was at this moment that Mr. Compton was called to the telephone in an adjoining room, and when he had gone the girl turned suddenly upon Jimmy Torrance. There was no cordiality nor friendship in her expression; a sneer upcurved her short upper lip.

"I do not wish to humiliate you unnecessarily in the presence of my father," she said. "You have managed to deceive him into believing that you are what you claim to be. Mr. Bince has known from the start that you are incompetent and incapable of accomplishing the results father thinks you are accomplishing. Now that you know that I know you to be an impostor, what do you intend to do?"

"I intend to keep right on with my work in the plant, Miss Compton," replied Jimmy.

"How long do you suppose father would keep you after I told him what I know of you? Do you think that he would for a moment place the future of his business in the hands of an ex-waiter from Feinheimer's—that he would let a milk-wagon driver tell him how to run his business?"

"It probably might make a difference," said Jimmy, "if he knew, but he will not know—listen, Miss Compton, I have discovered some things there that I have not even dared as yet to tell your father. The whole future of the business may depend upon my being there during the next few weeks. If I wasn't sure of what I am saying I might consider acceding to your demands rather than to embarrass you with certain knowledge which I have."

"You refuse to leave, then?" she demanded.

"I do," he said.

"Very well," she replied; "I shall tell father when he returns to this room just what I know of you."

"Will you tell him," asked Jimmy, "that you went to the training quarters of a prize-fighter, or that you dined unescorted at Feinheimer's at night and were an object of the insulting attentions of such a notorious character as Steve Murray?"

The girl flushed. "You would tell him that?" she demanded. "Oh, of course, I might have known that you would. It is difficult to realize that any one dining at my father's home is not a gentleman. I had forgotten for the moment."

"Yes," said Jimmy, "I would tell him, not from a desire to harm you, but because this is the only way that I can compel you to refrain from something that would result in inestimable harm to your father."

21

JIMMY TELLS THE TRUTH

MR. COMPTON returned to the room before Jimmy had discovered whether the girl intended to expose him or not. She said nothing about the matter during dinner, and immediately thereafter she excused herself, leaving the two men alone.

During the conversation that ensued Jimmy discovered that Bince had been using every argument at his command to induce Compton to let him go, as well as getting rid of the certified public accountants.

"I can't help but feel," said Compton, "that possibly there may be some reason in what Mr. Bince says, for he seems to feel more strongly on this subject than almost any question that has ever arisen in the plant wherein we differed, and it may be that I am doing wrong to absolutely ingore his wishes in the matter.

"As a matter of fact, Mr. Torrance, I have reached the point where I don't particularly relish a fight, as I did in the past. I would rather have things run along smoothly than to have this feeling of unrest and unpleasantness that now exists in the plant. I do not say that you are to blame for it, but the fact remains that ever since you came I have been constantly harassed by this same unpleasant condition which grows worse day by day. There is no question but what you have accomplished a great deal for us of a practical nature, but I believe in view of Mr. Bince's feelings in the matter that we had better terminate our arrangement."

Jimmy suddenly noted how old and tired his employer looked. He realized, too, that for a week he had been fighting an incipient influenza and that doubtless his entire mental attitude was influenced by the insidious workings of the disease, one of the marked symptoms of which he knew to be a feeling of despondency and mental depression, which sapped both courage and initiative.

They were passing through the hallway from the dining-room to the library, and as Compton concluded what was equivalent to Jimmy's discharge, he had stopped and turned toward the younger man. They were standing near the entrance to the music-room in which Elizabeth chanced to be, so that she overheard her father's words, and not without a smile of satisfaction and relief.

"Mr. Compton," replied Jimmy, "no matter what you do with me, you simply must not let those C.P.A.'s go until they have completed their work. I know something of what it is going to mean to your business, but I would rather that the reports come from them than from me."

"What do you mean?" asked Compton.

"I didn't want to be the one to tell you," replied

Jimmy. "I preferred that the C.P.A.'s discover it, as they will within the next day or two—you are being systematically robbed. I suspected it before I had been there ten days, and I was absolutely sure of it at the time I suggested you employ the C.P.A.'s. You are being robbed at the rate of approximately one thousand dollars a week."

"How?" asked Compton.

"I would rather you would wait for the report of the C.P.A.'s," returned Jimmy.

"I wish to know now," said Compton, "how I am being robbed."

Jimmy looked straight into the older man's eyes. "Through the pay-roll," he replied.

For a full minute Compton did not speak. "You may continue with your work in the plant," he said at last, "and we will keep the accountants, for a while at least. And now I am going to ask you to excuse me. I find that I tire very quickly since I have been threatened with influenza."

Jimmy bid his employer good night, and Mr. Compton turned into the library as the former continued along across the hall to the entrance. He was putting on his over-coat when Elizabeth Compton emerged from the music-room and approached him.

"I overheard your conversation with father," she said. "It seems to me that you are making a deliberate attempt to cause him worry and apprehension—you are taking advantage of his illness to frighten him into keeping you in his employ. I should think you would be ashamed of yourself."

"I am sorry that you think that," said Jimmy. "If it was not for your father and you I wouldn't have urged the matter at all."

"You are just doing it to hold your position," retorted the girl, "and now, by threats of blackmail you prevent me from exposing you—you are a despicable cur."

Jimmy felt the blood mounting to his face. He was mortified and angry, and yet he was helpless because his traducer was a woman. Unconsciously he drew himself to his full height.

"You will have to think about me as you please," he said; "I cannot influence that, but I want you to understand that you are not to interfere with my work. I think we understand one another perfectly, Miss Compton. Good night."

And as he closed the door behind him he left a very angry young lady biting her lower lip and almost upon the verge of angry tears.

"The boor," she exclaimed; "he dared to order me about and threaten me."

The telephone interrupted her unhappy train of thoughts. It was Bince.

"I am sorry, Elizabeth," he said, "but I won't be able to come up this evening. I have some important business to attend to. How is your father?"

"He seems very tired and despondent," replied Elizabeth. "That efficiency person was here to dinner. He just left."

She could not see the startled and angry expression of Bince's face as he received this information. "Torrance was there?" he asked. "How did that happen?"

"Father asked him to dinner, and when he wanted to discharge the fellow Torrance told him something that upset father terribly, and urged that he be kept a little while longer, to which father agreed."

"What did he tell him?" asked Bince.

"Oh, some alarmist tale about somebody robbing father. I didn't quite make out what it was all about, but it had something to do with the payroll."

Bince went white. "Don't believe anything that fellow says," he exclaimed excitedly; "he's nothing but a crook. Elizabeth, can't you make your father realize that he ought to get rid of the man, that he ought to leave things to me instead of trusting an absolute stranger?"

"I have," replied the girl, "and he was on the point of doing it until Torrance told him this story."

"Something will have to be done," said Bince, "at once. I'll be over to see your father in the morning. Good-by, dear," and he hung up the receiver.

After Jimmy left the Compton home he started to walk down-town. It was too early to go to his dismal little room on Indiana Avenue. The Lizard was still away. He had seen nothing of him for weeks, and with his going he had come to realize that he had rather depended upon the Lizard for company. He was full of interesting stories of the underworld and his dry humor and strange philosophy amused and entertained Jimmy.

And now as he walked along the almost deserted drive after his recent unpleasant scene with Elizabeth Compton he felt more blue and lonely than he had for many weeks. He craved human companionship, and so strong was the urge that his thoughts naturally turned to the only person other than the Lizard who seemed to have taken any particularly kindly interest in him. Acting on the impulse he turned west at the first cross street until he came to a drug-store. Entering a telephone-booth he called a certain number and a moment later had his connection.

"Is that you, Edith?" he asked, and at the affirmative reply, "this is Jimmy Torrance. I'm feeling terribly lonesome. I was wondering if I couldn't drag you out to listen to my troubles?"

"Surest thing you know," cried the girl. "Where are you?" He told her. "Take a Clark Street car," she told him, "and I'll be at the corner of North Avenue by the time you get there."

As the girl hung up the receiver and turned from the phone a slightly quizzical expression reflected some thought that was in her mind. "I wonder," she said as she returned to her room, "if he is going to be like the rest?"

She seated herself before her mirror and critically examined her reflection in the glass. She knew she was good-looking. No need of a mirror to tell her that. Her youth and her good looks had been her stock in trade, and yet this evening she appraised her features most critically, and as with light fingers she touched her hair, now in one place and now in another, she found herself humming a gay little tune and she realized that she was very happy.

When Jimmy Torrance alighted from the Clark Street car he found Edith waiting for him.

"It was mighty good of you," he said. "I don't know when I have had such a fit of blues, but I feel better already."

"What is the matter?" she asked.

"I just had a talk with Mr. Compton," he replied. "He sent for me and I had to tell him something that I didn't want to tell him, although he's got to find it out sooner or later anyway."

"Is there something wrong at the plant?" she asked.

"Wrong doesn't describe it," he exclaimed bitterly. "The man that he has done the most for and in whose loyalty he ought to have the right of implicit confidence, is robbing him blind."

"Bince?" asked the girl. Jimmy nodded. "I didn't like that pill," she said, "from the moment I saw him."

"Nor I," said Jimmy, "but he is going to marry Miss Compton and inherit the business. He's the last man in the place that Compton would suspect. It was just like suggesting to a man that his son was robbing him."

"Have you got the goods on him?" asked Edith.

"I will have as soon as the C. P. A.'s get to digging into the pay-roll," he replied, "and I just as good as got the information I need even without that. Well, let's forget our troubles. What shall we do?"

"What do you want to do?" she asked.

He could not tell by either her tone or expression with what anxiety she awaited his reply. "Suppose we do something exciting, like going to the movies," he suggested with a laugh.

"That suits me all right," said the girl. "There is a dandy comedy down at the Castle."

And so they went to the picture show, and when it was over he suggested that they have a bite to eat.

"I'll tell you," Edith suggested. "Suppose we go to Feinheimer's restaurant and see if we can't get that table that I used to eat at when you waited on me?" They both laughed.

"If old Feinheimer sees me he will have me poisoned," said Jimmy.

"Not if you have any money to spend in his place."

It was eleven thirty when they reached Feinheimer's. The table they wanted was vacant, a little table in a corner of the room and furthest from the orchestra. The waiter, a new man, did not know them, and no one had recognized them as they entered.

Jimmy sat looking at the girl's profile as she studied the menu-card. She was very pretty. He had always thought her that, but somehow to-night she seemed to be different, even more beautiful than in the past. He wished that he could forget what she had been. And he realized as he looked at her sweet girlish face upon which vice had left no slightest impression to mark her familiarity with vice, that it might be easy to forget her past. And then between him and the face of the girl before him arose the vision of another face, the face of the girl that he had set upon a pedestal and worshiped from afar. And with the recollection of her came a realization of the real cause of his sorrow and depression earlier in the evening.

He had attributed it to the unpleasant knowledge he had been forced to partially impart to her father and also in some measure to the regrettable interview he had had with her, but now he knew that these were only contributory causes, that the real reason was that during the months she had occupied his thoughts and in the few meetings he had had with her there had developed within him, unknown to himself, a sentiment for her that could be described by but one word—love.

Always, though he had realized that she was unattainable, there must have lingered within his breast a faint spark of hope that somehow, some time, there would be a chance, but after to-night he knew there could never be a chance. She had openly confessed her contempt for him, and how would she feel later when she realized that through his efforts her happiness was to be wrecked, and the man she loved and was to marry branded as a criminal?

Part Four

22

A LETTER FROM MURRAY

THE girl opposite him looked up from the card before her. The lines of her face were softened by the suggestion of a contented smile. "My gracious!" she exclained. "What's the matter now? You look as though you had lost your last friend."

Jimmy quickly forced a smile to his lips. "On the contrary," he said, "I think I've found a regular friend—in you."

It was easy to see that his words pleased her.

"No," continued Jimmy; "I was thinking of what an awful mess I make of everything I tackle."

"You're not making any mess of this new job," she said. "You're making good. You see, my hunch was all right."

"I wish you hadn't had your hunch," he said with a smile. "It's going to bring a lot of trouble to several people, but now that I'm in it I'm going to stick to it to a finish."

The girl's eyes were wandering around the room, taking in the faces of the diners about them. Suddenly she extended her hand and laid it on Jimmy's.

"For the love of Mike!" she exclaimed. "Look over there."

Slowly Jimmy turned his eyes in the direction she indicated.

"What do you know about that?" he ejaculated. "Steve Murray and Bince!"

"And thick as thieves," said the girl.

"Naturally," commented Jimmy.

The two men left the restaurant before Edith and Jimmy had finished their supper, leaving the two hazarding various guesses as to the reason for their meeting.

"You can bet it's for no good," said the girl. "I've known Murray for a long while, and I never knew him to do a decent thing in his life."

Their supper over, they walked to Clark Street and took a northbound car, but after alighting Jimmy walked with the girl to the entrance of her apartment.

"I can't thank you enough," he said, "for giving me this evening. It is the only evening I have enjoyed since I struck this town last July."

He unlocked the outer door for her and was holding it open.

"It is I who ought to thank you," she said. Her voice was very low and filled with suppressed feeling. "I ought to thank you, for this has been the happiest evening of my life," and as though she could not trust herself to say more, she entered the hallway and closed the door between them.

As Jimmy turned away to retrace his steps to the

car-line he found his mind suddenly in a whirl of jumbled emotions, for he was not so stupid as to have failed to grasp something of the significance of the girl's words and manner.

"Hell!" he muttered. "Look what I've done now!"

The girl hurried to her room and turned on the lights, and again she seated herself before her mirror, and for a moment sat staring at the countenance reflected before her. She saw lips parted to rapid breathing, lips that curved sweetly in a happy smile, and then as she sat there looking she saw the expression of the face before her change. The lips ceased to smile, the soft, brown eyes went wide and staring as though in sudden horror. For a moment she sat thus and then, throwing her body forward upon her dressing-table, she buried her face in her arms.

"My God!" she cried through choking sobs.

Mason Compton was at his office the next morning, contrary to the pleas of his daughter and the orders of his physician. Bince was feeling more cheerful. Murray had assured him that there was a way out. He would not tell Bince what the way was.

"Just leave it to me," he said. "The less you know, the better off you'll be. What you want is to get rid of this fresh guy and have all the papers in a certain vault destroyed. You see to it that only the papers you want destroyed are in that vault, and I'll do the rest."

All of which relieved Mr. Harold Bince's elastic conscience of any feeling of responsibility in the matter. Whatever Murray did was no business of his. He was glad that Murray hadn't told him.

He greeted Jimmy Torrance almost affably, but he lost something of his self-composure when Mason Compton arrived at the office, for Bince had been sure that his employer would be laid up for at least another week, during which time Murray would have completed his work.

The noon mail brought a letter from Murray.

"Show the enclosed to Compton," it read. "Tell him you found it on your desk, and destroy this letter." The enclosure was a crudely printed note on a piece of soiled wrapping-paper:

TREAT YOUR MEN RIGHT OR SUFFER THE CONSEQUENCES

I.W.W.

Bince laid Murray's letter face down upon the balance of the open mail, and sat for a long time looking at the ominous words of the enclosure. At first he was inclined to be frightened, but finally a crooked smile twisted his lips. "Murray's not such a fool, after all," he soliloquized. "He's framing an alibi before he starts."

With the note in his hand, Bince entered Compton's office, where he found the latter dictating to Edith Hudson. "Look at this thing!" exclaimed Bince, laying the note before Compton. "What do you suppose it means?"

Compton read it, and his brows knitted. "Have the men been complaining at all?" he asked.

"Recently I have heard a little grumbling," replied Bince. "They haven't taken very kindly to

Torrance's changes, and I guess some of them are afraid they are going to lose their jobs, as they know he is cutting down the force in order to cut costs."

"He ought to know about this," said Compton. "Wait; I'll have him in," and he pressed a button on his desk. A moment later Jimmy entered, and Compton showed him the note.

"What do you think of it?" asked Compton.

"I doubt if it amounts to much," replied Jimmy. "The men have no grievance. It may be the work of some fellow who was afraid of his job, but I doubt if it really emanates from any organized scheme of intimidation. If I were you, sir, I would simply ignore it."

To Jimmy's surprise, Bince agreed with him. It was the first time that Bince had agreed with anything Jimmy had suggested.

"Very well," assented Compton, "but we'll preserve this bit of evidence in case we may need it later," and he handed the slip of paper to Edith Hudson. "File this, please, Miss Hudson," he said; and then, turning to Bince:

"It may be nothing, but I don't like the idea of it. There is apt to be something underlying this, or even if it is only a single individual and he happens to be a crank he could cause a lot of trouble. Suppose, for instance, one of these crack-brained foreigners in the shop got it into his head that Torrance here was grinding him down in order to increase our profits? Why, he might attack him at any time! I tell you, we have got to be prepared for such a contingency, especially now that we have concrete evidence that there is such a man in our employ. I think you ought to be armed, Mr. Torrance. Have you a pistol?"

Jimmy shook his head negatively.

"No, sir," he said; "not here."

Compton opened a desk drawer.

"Take this one," he said, and handed Jimmy an automatic.

The latter smiled. "Really, Mr. Compton," he said, "I don't believe I need such an article."

"I want you to take it," insisted Compton. "I want you to be on the safe side."

A moment later Bince and Jimmy left the office together. Jimmy still carried the pistol in his hand.

"You'd better put that thing in your pocket," cautioned Bince.

They were in the small office on which Compton's and Bince's offices opened, and Jimmy had stopped beside the desk that had been placed there for him.

"I think I'll leave it here," he said. "The thing would be a nuisance in my pocket," and he dropped it into one of the desk drawers, while Bince continued his way toward the shop.

Compton was looking through the papers and letters on his desk, evidently searching for something which he could not find, while the girl sat awaiting for him to continue his dictation.

"That's funny," commented Compton. "I was certain that that letter was here. Have you seen anything of a letter from Mosher."

"No, sir," replied Edith.

"Well, I wish you would step into Mr. Bince's

office, and see if it is on his desk."

Upon the assistant general manager's desk lay a small pile of papers, face down, which Edith proceeded to examine in search of the Mosher letter. She had turned them all over at once, commencing at what had previously been the bottom of the pile, so that she ran through them all without finding the Mosher letter before she came to Murray's epistle.

As its import dawned upon her, her eyes widened at first in surprise and then narrowed as she realized the value of her discovery. At first she placed the letter back with the others just as she had found them, but on second thought she took it up quickly and, folding it, slipped it inside her waist. Then she returned to Compton's office.

"I cannot find the Mosher letter," she said.

23

LAID UP

HARRIET HOLDEN was sitting in Elizabeth's boudoir.
"And he had the effrontery," the latter was saying, "to tell me what I must do and must not do! The idea! A miserable little milk-wagon driver dictating to me!"

Miss Holden smiled.

"I should not call him very little," she remarked.

"I didn't mean physically," retorted Elizabeth. "It is absolutely insufferable. I am going to demand that father discharge the man."

"And suppose he asks you why?" asked Harriet. "You will tell him, of course, that you want this person discharged because he protected you from the insults and attacks of a ruffian while you were dining in Feinheimer's at night—is that it?"

"You are utterly impossible, Harriet!" cried Elizabeth, stamping her foot. "You are as bad as that efficiency person. But, then, I might have expected it! You have always, it seems to me, shown a great deal more interest in the fellow than necessary, and probably the fact that Harold doesn't like him is enough to make you partial toward him, for you have never tried to hide the fact that you don't like Harold."

"If you're going to be cross," said Harriet, "I think I shall go home."

At about the same time the Lizard entered Feinheimer's. In the far corner of the room Murray was seated at a table. The Lizard approached and sat down opposite him. "Here I am," he said. "What do you want, and how did you know I was in town?"

"I didn't know," said Murray. "I got a swell job for you, and so I sent out word to get you."

"You're in luck then," said the Lizard. "I just blew in this morning. What kind of a job you got?"

Murray explained at length.

"They got a watchman," he concluded, "but I've got a guy on de inside that'll fix him."

"When do I pull this off?" asked the Lizard.

"In about a week. I'll let you know the night later. Dey ordinarily draw the pay-roll money Monday, the same day dey pay, but dis week they'll draw it Saturday and leave it in the safe. It'll be layin' on top of a bunch of books and papers. Dey're de t'ings you're to destroy. As I told you, it will all be fixed from de inside. Dere's no danger of a pinch. All you gotta do is crack de safe, put about a four or five t'ousand dollar roll in your pocket, and as you cross de river drop a handful of books and papers in. Nothin' to it—it's the easiest graft you ever had."

"You're sure dat's all?" asked the Lizard.

"Sure thing!" replied Murray.

"Where's de place?"

"Dat I can't tell you until the day we're ready to pull off de job."

At four o'clock that afternoon Jimmy Torrance collapsed at his desk. The flu had struck him as suddenly and as unexpectedly as it had attacked many of its victims. Edith Hudson found him, and immediately notified Mr. Compton, with the result that half an hour later Jimmy Torrance was in a small private hospital in Park Avenue.

That night Bince got Murray over the phone. He told him of Jimmy's sickness.

"He's balled up the whole plan," he complained. "We've either got to wait until he croaks or is out again before we can go ahead, unless something else arises to make it necessary to act before. I think I can hold things off, though, at this end, all right."

For four or five days Jimmy was a pretty sick man. He was allowed to see no one, but even if Jimmy had been in condition to give the matter any thought he would not have expected to see any one, for who was there to visit him in the hospital, who was there who knew of his illness, to care whether he was sick or well, alive or dead? It was on the fifth day that Jimmy commenced to take notice of anything. At Compton's orders he had been placed in a private room and given a special nurse, and to-day for the first time he learned of Mr. Compton's kindness and the fact that the nurse was instructed to call Jimmy's employer twice a day and report the patient's condition.

"Mighty nice of him," thought Jimmy, and then

to the nurse: "And the flowers, too? Does he send those?"

The young woman shook her head negatively.

"No," she said; "a young lady comes every evening about six and leaves the flowers. She always asks about your condition and when she may see you."

Jimmy was silent for some time. "She comes every evening?" he asked.

"Yes," replied the nurse.

"May I see her this evening?" asked Jimmy.

"We'll ask the doctor," she replied; and the doctor must have given consent, for at six o'clock that evening the nurse brought Edith Hudson to his bedside.

The girl came every evening thereafter and sat with Jimmy as long as the nurse would permit her to remain. Jimmy discovered during those periods a new side to her character, a mothering tenderness that filled him with a feeling of content and happiness the moment that she entered the room, and which doubtless aided materially in his rapid convalescence, for until she had been permitted to see him Jimmy had suffered as much from mental depression as from any other of the symptoms of his disease.

He had felt utterly alone and uncared for, and in this mental state he had brooded over his failures to such an extent that he had reached a point where he felt that death would be something of a relief. Militating against his recovery had been the parting words of Elizabeth Compton the evening that he had dined at her father's home, but now all that was very nearly forgotten—at least crowded into the dim vistas of recollection by the unselfish friendship of this girl of the streets.

Jimmy's nurse quite fell in love with Edith.

"She is such a sweet girl," she said, "and always so cheerful. She is going to make some one a mighty good wife," and she smiled knowingly at Jimmy.

The suggestion which her words implied came to Jimmy as a distinct shock. He had never thought of Edith Hudson in the light of this suggestion, and now he wondered if there could be any such sentiment as it implied in Edith's heart, but finally he put the idea away with a shrug.

"Impossible," he thought. "She thinks of me as I think of her, only as a good friend."

24

IN THE TOILS

AT the office of the International Machine Company the work of the C. P. A.'s was drawing to a close. Their report would soon be ready to submit to Mr. Compton, and as the time approached Bince's nervousness and irritability increased. Edith noticed that he inquired each day with growing solicitude as to the reports from the hospital relative to Jimmy's condition. She knew that Bince disliked Jimmy, and yet the man seemed strangely anxious for his recovery and return to work.

In accordance with Jimmy's plan, the C. P. A.'s were to give out no information to any one, even to Mr. Compton, until their investigation and report were entirely completed. This plan had been approved by Mr. Compton, although he professed to be at considerable loss to understand why it was necessary. It was, however, in accordance with Jimmy's plan to prevent, if possible, any interference with the work of the auditors until every available fact in the case had been ascertained and recorded.

In the investigation of the pay-roll Bince had worked diligently with the accountants. As a matter of fact, he had never left them a moment while the pay-roll records were in their hands, and had gone to much pain to explain in detail every question arising therefrom.

Although the investigators seemed to accept his statements at their face value, the assistant general manager was far from being assured that their final report would redound to his credit.

On a Thursday they informed him that they had completed their investigation, and the report would be submitted to Mr. Compton on Saturday.

When Edith reached the hospital that evening she found Jimmy in high spirits. He was dressed for the first time, and assured her that he was quite able to return to work if the doctor would let him, but the nurse shook her head. "You ought to stay here for another week or ten days," she admonished him.

"Nothing doing," cried Jimmy. "I'll be out of here Monday at the latest." But when Edith told him that the C. P. A.'s had finished, and that their report would be handed in Saturday, Jimmy announced that he would leave the hospital the following day.

"But you can't do it," said the nurse.

"Why not?" asked Jimmy.

"The doctor won't permit it."

Edith tried to dissuade him, but he insisted that

it was absolutely necessary for him to be at the office when the C. P. A.'s report was made.

"I'll be over there Friday evening or Saturday morning at the latest," he said as she bid him good-by.

And so it was that, despite the pleas of his nurse and the orders of his physician, Jimmy appeared at the plant Friday afternoon. Bince greeted him almost effusively, and Mr. Compton seemed glad to see him out again.

That evening Harold Bince met Murray at Feinheimer's, and still later the Lizard received word that Murray wanted to see him.

"Everything's ready," the boss explained to the Lizard. "The whole thing's framed for to-morrow night. The watchman was discharged to-day. Another man is supposed to have been hired to take the job, but of course he won't show up. You meet me here at seven thirty to-morrow night, and I'll give you your final instructions and tell you how to get to the plant."

The C. P. A.'s were slow in completing their report. At noon on Saturday it looked very much to Bince that there would be no report ready before Monday. He had spent most of the forenoon pacing his office, and at last, unable longer to stand the strain, he had announced that he was going out to his country club for a game of golf.

He returned to his down-town club about dinner-time, and at eight o'clock he called up Elizabeth Compton.

"Come on up," said the girl. "I'm all alone this evening. Father went back to the office to examine some reports that were just finished up late this afternoon."

"I'll be over," said Bince, "as soon as I dress." If there was any trace of surprise or shock in his tones the girl failed to notice it.

At ten o'clock that night a figure moved silently through the dark shadows of an alleyway in the rear of the International Machine Company's plant on West Superior Street. As he moved along he counted the basement windows silently, and at the fifth window he halted. Just a casual glance he cast up and down the alley, and then, kneeling, he raised the sash and slipped quietly into the darkness of the basement.

At about the same time Jimmy's land-lady called him to the telephone, where a man's voice asked if "this was Mr. Torrance?" Assured that such was the fact, the voice continued: "I am the new watchman at the plant. There's something wrong here. I can't get hold of Mr. Compton. I think you better come down. I'll be in Mr. Compton's office—" The message ceased as though central had disconnected them.

"Funny," thought Jimmy, "that he should call me up. I wonder what the trouble can be." But he lost no time in getting his hat and starting for the works.

Although the Lizard knew that there was no danger of detection, yet from long habit he moved through the plant of the International Machine Company with the noiselessness of a disembodied spirit. Occasionally, and just for the briefest instant, he flashed his lamp ahead of him, but though he had never been in the place before he found it scarcely necessary, so minute had been his instructions for reaching the office from the fifth basement window.

The room he sought was on the second floor, and the Lizard had mounted the steps from the basement to the first floor when he was brought to a sudden stop by a noise from the floor above him. The Lizard listened intently. No, he could not be mistaken. Too often had he heard a similar sound.

Some one was tiptoeing across the floor above. The Lizard was in the hallway close beside the stairs when he realized the footsteps were coming toward the stairway, and a moment later that they were cautiously descending. The Lizard flattened himself against the wall, and if he breathed his lungs gave forth no sound.

If one may interpret footsteps—and the Lizard, from the fund of a great experience, felt that he could—those descending the stairway from above him might have been described as nervous and repressed; for at least they gave the Lizard the impression of one who desired to flee in haste and yet dared not do so, for fear of attracting attention by the increased noise that greater speed might entail.

At least the Lizard knew that those were the footsteps of no watchman, but whether it be guardian of the law or fellow criminal the Lizard had no wish to be discovered. He wondered what had gone wrong with Murray's plans, and, suddenly imbued with the natural suspicion of the criminal, it occurred to him that the whole thing might be a frame-up to get him; and yet why Murray should wish to get him he could not imagine. He ran over in his mind a list of those who might feel enmity toward him, but among them all the Lizard could cast upon none who might have sufficient against him to warrant such an elaborate scheme of revenge.

The footsteps passed him and continued on toward the foot of the stairs where was the main entrance which opened upon the street. At the door the footsteps halted, and as the Lizard's eyes bored through the darkness in the direction of the other prowler the latter struck a match upon the panel of the door and lighted a cigarette, revealing his features momentarily but distinctly to the watcher in the shadow of the stairway. Then he opened the door and passed out into the night.

The Lizard, listening intently for a few moments to assure himself that there was no one else above, and that the man who had just departed was not returning, at last continued his way to the foot of the stairs, which he ascended to the second floor. Passing through the outer office, he paused a moment before the door to Compton's private office, and then silently turning the knob he gently pushed the door open and stepped into the room.

Beyond the threshold he halted and pressed the button of his flash-lamp. For just an instant its faint rays illumined the interior of the room, and then darkness blotted out the scene. But whatever it was that the little flash-lamp had revealed was evidently in the nature of a surprise, and perhaps something of a shock, to the Lizard, for he drew back with a muttered oath, backed quietly out of the room, closed the door after him, and, moving much more swiftly than he had entered, retraced his steps to the fifth window on the alley, and was gone from the scene with whatever job he had contemplated unexecuted.

A half-hour later detective headquarters at the Central Station received an anonymous tip: "Send some one to the office of the International Machine Company, on the second floor of —— West Superior Street."

It was ten thirty when Jimmy reached the plant. He entered the front door with his own latchkey, pressed the button which lighted the stairway and the landing above, and, ascending, went straight to Mr. Compton's office, turned the knob, and opened the door, to find that the interior was dark.

"Strange," he thought, "that after sending for me the fellow didn't wait." As these thoughts passed through his mind he fumbled on the wall for the switch, and, finding it, flooded the office with light.

As he turned again toward the room he voiced a sudden exclamation of horror, for on the floor beside his desk lay the body of Mason Compton! As Jimmy stepped quickly toward Compton's body and kneeled beside it a man tiptoed quietly up the front stairway, while another, having ascended from the rear, was crossing the outer office with equal stealth.

Jimmy felt of Compton's face and hands. They were warm. And then he placed his ear close against the man's breast, in order to see if he could detect the beating of the heart. He was in this position when he was startled by a gruff voice behind him.

"Put 'em up!" it admonished curtly, and Jimmy turned to see two men standing in the doorway with pistols leveled at him.

25
CIRCUMSTANTIAL EVIDENCE

AT first Jimmy thought they were the perpetrators of the deed, but almost immediately he recognized one of them as O'Donnell, the erstwhile traffic officer who had been promoted to a detective sergeancy since Jimmy had first met him.

"Compton has been murdered," said Jimmy dully. "He is dead."

"Put up your hands," snapped O'Donnell for the second time, "and be quick about it!"

It was then for the first time that Jimmy realized the meaning that might be put upon his presence alone in the office with his dead employer. O'Donnell's partner searched him, but found no weapon upon him.

"Where's the gat?" he asked.

"Whoever did this probably took it with him," said Jimmy. "Find the watchman."

They made Jimmy sit down in a corner, and while one of them guarded him the other called up central, made his report, and asked for an ambulance and the wagon. Then O'Donnell commenced to examine the room. A moment later he found an automatic behind the door across the room from where Compton's body lay.

"Ever see this before?" asked O'Donnell, holding the pistol up to Jimmy.

"If you're asking me if it's mine, no," said Jimmy. "I have a gun, but it's home. I never carry it. I didn't do this, O'Donnell," he continued. "There was no reason why I should do it, so instead of wasting your time on me while the murderer escapes you'd better get busy on some other theory, too. It won't do any harm, anyway."

The wagon came and took Jimmy to the station, and later he was questioned by the lieutenant in charge.

"You say this is not your pistol?" asked the police officer.

"It is not," replied Jimmy.

"You never saw it before?"

"No, I have not."

The lieutenant turned to one of his men, who went to the door, and, opening it, returned almost immediately with Bince.

"Do you know this man, Mr. Bince?" asked the lieutenant.

"I certainly do," said Bince.

"Did you ever see this pistol before?"

Bince took the weapon and examined it. "Yes," he said.

"Under what circumstances?" asked the lieutenant.

"It was one of two that Mr. Compton had in his desk. This one he loaned to Torrance two or three weeks ago. I was in the office at the time."

The officer turned toward Jimmy.

"Now do you recognize it?" he asked.

"I haven't denied," said Jimmy, "that Mr. Compton had loaned me a pistol. As a matter of fact, I had forgotten all about it. I do not particularly recognize this one as the weapon he loaned me, though it is of the same type. There is no way that I could identify the particular weapon he handed me."

"But you admit he loaned you one?"

"Yes," said Jimmy.

"What did you do with it?" asked the policeman.

"I put it in my desk within five minutes after he gave it to me, and I haven't seen it since."

"You say you couldn't identify the pistol?" said the officer.

Jimmy nodded.

"Well, we can, and have. The number of this pistol was recorded when Mr. Compton bought it, as was the number of the other one which is still in his desk. They were the only two pistols he ever bought, according to Mr. Bince, and his daughter, aside from one which he had at home, which has also been accounted for. The drawer in which Mr. Bince saw you place this pistol we found open and the pistol gone. It looks pretty bad for you, young fellow, and if you want a chance to dodge the rope you'd better plead guilty and tell us why you did it."

Jimmy was given little opportunity for sleep that night. A half-dozen times he was called back to the lieutenant's office for further questioning. He commenced to realize that the circumstantial evidence was strongly against him, and now, as the girl had warned him, his entirely innocent past was brought up against him simply because his existence had been called to the attention of a policeman, and the same policeman an inscrutable Fate had ordained should discover him alone with a murdered man.

O'Donnell made the most of his meager knowledge of Jimmy. He told the lieutenant with embellishments of Jimmy's association with such characters as the Lizard and Little Eva; but the police were still at a loss to discover a motive.

This, however, was furnished the next morning, when Elizabeth Compton, white and heavy-eyed, was brought to the station to identify Jimmy. There was deep compassion in the young man's face as he was ushered into the presence of the stricken girl, while at sight of him her's mirrored horror, contempt, and hatred.

"You know this man?" asked the lieutenant.

"Yes," she replied. "His name is Torrance. I have seen him a number of times in the past year. He worked as a clerk in a store, in the hosiery department, and waited on me there. Later I"—she hesitated—"I saw him in a place called Feinheimer's. He was a waiter. Then he was a sparring partner, I think they call it, for a prizefighter. Some of my friends took me to a gymnasium to see the fighter training, and I recognized this man.

"I saw him again when he was driving a milk-wagon. He delivered milk at a friend's house where I chanced to be. The last time I saw him was at my father's home. He had obtained employment in my father's plant as an efficiency expert. He seemed to exercise some strange power over father, who believed implicitly in him, until recently, when he evidently commenced to have doubts; for the night that the man was at our house I was sitting in the music-room when they passed through the hallway, and I heard father discharge him. But the fellow pleaded to be retained, and finally father promised to keep him for a while longer, as I recall it, at least until certain work was completed at the plant. This work was completed yesterday. That's all I know. I do not know whether father discharged him again or not."

Harriet Holden had accompanied her friend to the police station, and was sitting close beside her during the examination, her eyes almost constantly upon the face of the prisoner. She saw no fear there, only an expression of deep-seated sorrow for her friend.

The lieutenant was still asking questions when there came a knock at the door, which was immediately opened, revealing O'Donnell with a young woman, whom he brought inside.

"I guess we're getting to the bottom of it," announced the sergeant. "Look who I found workin' over there as Compton's stenographer."

"Well, who is she?" demanded the lieutenant.

"A jane who used to hang out at Feinheimer's. She has been runnin' around with this bird. They tell me over there that Compton hired her on this fellow's recommendation. Get hold of the Lizard now, and you'll have the whole bunch."

Thus did Sergeant Patrick O'Donnell solve the

entire mystery with Sherlockian ease and despatch.

At Jimmy's preliminary hearing he was held to the grand jury, and on the strength of the circumstantial evidence against him that body voted a true bill. Edith Hudson, against whom there was no evidence of any nature, was held as a witness for the State, and a net was thrown out for the Lizard which dragged in nearly every pickpocket in town except the man they sought.

Jimmy had been in jail for about a week when he received a visitor. A turnkey brought her to his cell. It was Harriet Holden. She greeted him seriously but pleasantly, and then she asked the turnkey if she might go inside.

"It's against the rules, miss," he said, "but I guess it will be all right." He recalled that the sheriff had said that the girl's father was a friend of his, and so he assumed that it would be safe to relax the rules in her behalf. He had been too long an employee of the county not to know that rules are often elastic to the proper pressure.

"I have been wanting to talk to you," said the girl to Jimmy, "ever since this terrible thing happened. Somehow I cannot believe that you are guilty, and there must be some way in which you can prove your innocence."

"I have been trying to think out how I might," said Jimmy, "but the more I think about it the more damning the circumstantial evidence against me appears."

"There must always be a motive for a crime like that," said Harriet. "I cannot believe that a simple fear of his discharge would be sufficient motive for any man to kill his employer."

"Not to kill a man who had been as good to me as Mr. Compton was," said Jimmy, "or a man whom I admired so much as I did him. As a matter of fact, he was not going to discharge me, Miss Holden, and I had an opportunity there for a very successful future; but now that he is dead there is no one who could verify such a statement on my part."

"Who could there be, then, who might wish to kill him, and what could the motive be?"

"I can only think," said Jimmy, "of one man; and even in his case the idea is too horrible—too preposterous to be entertained."

Harriet Holden looked up at him quickly, a sudden light in her eyes, and an expression of almost horrified incredulity upon her face. "You don't mean—" she started.

"I wouldn't even use his name in connection with the thought," Jimmy interrupted; "but he is the only man of whom I know who could have profited by Mr. Compton's death, and, on the other hand, whose entire future would have been blasted possibly had Mr. Compton lived until the following morning."

The girl remained for half an hour longer, and when she left she went directly to the home of Elizabeth Compton.

"I told you, Elizabeth," she said, "that I was going to see Mr. Torrance. You dissuaded me for some time, but I finally went to-day, and I am glad that I went. No one except yourself could have loved your father more than I, or have been more horrified or grieved at his death; but that is no reason why you should aid in the punishment of an innocent man, as I am confident that this man Torrance is, and I tell you Elizabeth if you were not prejudiced you would agree with me.

"I have talked with Torrance for over half an hour to-day, and since then nothing can ever make me believe that that man could commit a cold-blooded murder. Harold has always hated him—you admit that yourself—and now you are permitting him to prejudice you against the man purely on the strength of that dislike. I am going to help him. I'm going to do it, not only to obtain justice for him, but to assist in detecting and punishing the true murderer."

"I don't see, Harriet, how you can take any interest in such a creature," said Elizabeth. "You know from the circumstances under which we saw him before father employed him what type of man he is, and it was further exemplified by the evidence of his relationship with that common woman of the streets."

"He told me about her to-day," replied Harriet. "He had only known her very casually, but she helped him once—loaned him some money when he needed it—and when he found that she had been a stenographer and wanted to give up the life she had been leading and be straight again, he helped her.

"I asked Sergeant O'Donnell particularly about that, and even he had to admit that there was no evidence whatever to implicate the girl or show that the relations between her and Mr. Torrance had been anything that was not right; and you know yourself how anxious O'Donnell has been to dig up evidence of any kind derogatory to either of them."

"How are you going to help him?" asked Elizabeth. "Take flowers and cake to him in jail?"

There was a sneer on her face and on her lips.

"If he cares for flowers and cakes," replied Harriet, "I probably shall; but I have another plan which will probably be more practical."

26

"THE ONLY FRIENDS HE HAS"

SO it befell that the next day a well-known criminal attorney called on Jimmy Torrance at the county jail. "I understand," he said to Jimmy, "that you have retained no attorney. I have been instructed by one of my clients to take your case."

Jimmy looked at him in silence for a moment.

"Who is going to pay you?" he asked with a smile. "I understand attorneys expect to be paid."

"That needn't worry you." replied the lawyer.

"You mean that your client is going to pay for my defense? What's his name?"

"That I am not permitted to tell you," replied the lawyer.

"Very well. Tell your client that I appreciate his kindness, but I cannot accept it."

"Don't be a fool," said the attorney. "This client of mine can well afford the expense, and anyway, my instructions are to defend you whether you want me to or not, so I guess you can't help yourself."

Jimmy laughed with the lawyer. "All right," he

said. "The first thing I wish you'd do is to get Miss Hudson out of jail. There is doubtless some reason for suspicion attaching to me because I was found alone with Mr. Compton's body, and the pistol with which he was shot was one that had been given to me and which I kept in my desk, but there is no earthly reason why she should be detained. She could have had absolutely nothing to do with it."

"I will see what can be done," replied the attorney, "although I had no instructions to defend her also."

"I will make that one of the conditions under which I will accept your services," said Jimmy.

The result was that within a few days Edith was released. From the moment that she left the jail she was aware that she was being shadowed.

"I suppose," she thought, "that they expect to open up a fund of new clues through me," but she was disturbed nevertheless, because she realized that it was going to make difficult a thing that she had been trying to find some means to accomplish ever since she had been arrested.

She went directly to her apartment and presently took down the telephone-receiver, and after calling a public phone in a building down-town, she listened intently while the operator was getting her connection and before the connection was made she hung up the receiver with a smile, for she had distinctly heard the sound of a man's breathing over the line, and she knew that in all probability O'Donnell had tapped in immediately on learning that she had been released from jail.

That evening she attended a local motion-picture

theater which she often frequented. It was one of those small affairs, the width of a city block, with a narrow aisle running down either side and an emergency exit upon the alley at the far end of each aisle. The theater was darkened when she entered and, a quick glance apprizing her that no one followed her in immediately, she continued on down one of the side aisles and passed through the doorway into the alley.

Five minutes later she was in a telephone-booth in a drug-store two blocks away.

"Is this Feinheimer's?" she asked after she had got her connection. "I want to talk to Carl." She asked for Carl because she knew that this man who had been head-waiter at Feinheimer's for years would know her voice.

"Is that you, Carl?" she asked as a man's voice finally answered the telephone. "This is Little Eva."

"Oh, hello!" said the man. "I thought you were over at the county jail."

"I was released to-day," she explained. "Well, listen, Carl; I've got to see the Lizard. I've simply got to see him to-night. I was being shadowed, but I got away from them. Do you know where he is?"

"I guess I could find him," said Carl in a low voice. "You go out to Mother Kruger's. I'll tell him you'll be there in about an hour."

"I'll be waiting in a taxi outside," said the girl.

"Good," said Carl. "If he isn't there in an hour you can know that he was afraid to come. He's layin' pretty low."

"All right," said the girl, "I'll be there. You tell

him that he simply must come." She hung up the receiver and then called a taxi. She gave a number on a side street about a half block away, where she knew it would be reasonably dark, and consequently less danger of detection.

Three-quarters of an hour later her taxi drew up beside Mother Kruger's, but the girl did not alight. She had waited but a short time when another taxi swung in beside the road-house, turned around and backed up alongside hers. A man stepped out and peered through the glass of her machine. It was the Lizard.

Recognizing the girl he opened the door and took a seat beside her. "Well," inquired the Lizard, "what's on your mind?"

"Jimmy," replied the girl.

"I thought so," returned the Lizard. "It looks pretty bad for him, don't it? I wish there was some way to help him."

"He did not do it," said the girl.

"It didn't seem like him," said the Lizard, "but I got it straight from a guy who knows that he done it all right."

"Who?" asked Edith.

"Murray."

"I thought he knew a lot about it," said the girl. "That's why I sent for you. You haven't got any love for Murray, have you?"

"No," replied the Lizard; "not so you could notice it."

"I think Murray knows a lot about that job. If you want to help Jimmy I know where you can get the dope that will start something, anyway."

"What is it?" asked the Lizard.

"This fellow Bince, who is assistant general manager for Compton, got a letter from Murray two or three weeks before Compton was killed. Murray enclosed a threat signed I. W. W., and his letter instructed Bince to show the threat to Compton. I haven't got all the dope on it, but I've got a hunch that in some way it is connected with this job. Anyway, I've got both Murray's letter and the threat he enclosed. They're hidden in my desk at the plant. I can't get them, of course; they wouldn't let me in the place now, and Murray's so strong with the police that I wouldn't trust them, so I haven't told any one. What I want is for you to go there tonight and get them."

The Lizard was thinking fast. The girl knew nothing of his connection with the job. She did not know that he had entered Compton's office and had been first to find his dead body; in fact, no one knew that. Even Murray did not know that the Lizard had succeeded in entering the plant, as the latter had told him that he was delayed, and that when he reached there a patrol and ambulance were already backed up in front of the building. He felt that he had enough knowledge, however, to make the conviction of Jimmy a very difficult proposition, but if he divulged the knowledge he had and explained how he came by it he could readily see that suspicion would be at once transferred from Jimmy to himself.

The Lizard therefore was in a quandry. Of course, if Murray's connection was ever discovered the Lizard might then be drawn into it, but if he could keep Murray out the Lizard would be reasonably safe from suspicion, and now the girl had shown him how he might remove a damaging piece of evidence against Murray.

"You will get it, won't you?" asked the girl.

"Where are these papers?" he asked.

"They are in the outer office which adjoins Mr. Compton's. My desk stands at the right of the door as you enter from the main office. Remove the right-hand lower drawer and you will find the papers lying on the little wooden partition directly underneath the drawer."

"All right," said the Lizard; "I'll get them."

"Bless you, Lizard," cried the girl. "I knew you would help. You and I are the only friends he has. If we went back on him he'd be sent up, for there's lots of money being used against him. He might even be hanged. I know from what I have heard that the prosecuting attorney intends to ask for the death penalty."

The Lizard made no reply as he started to leave the taxi.

"Take them to his attorney," said the girl, and she gave him the name and address.

The Lizard grunted and entered his own cab. As he did so a man on a motorcycle drew up on the opposite side and peered through the window. The driver had started his motor as the newcomer approached. From her cab the girl saw the Lizard and the man on the motorcycle look into each other's face for a moment, then she heard the Lizard's quick admonition to his driver, "Beat it, bo!"

A sharp "Halt!" came from the man on the motorcycle, but the taxicab leaped forward, and, accelerating rapidly, turned to the left into the road toward the city. The girl had guessed at the first glance that the man on the motorcycle was a police officer. As the Lizard's taxi raced away the officer circled quickly and started in pursuit. "No chance," thought the girl. "He'll get caught sure." She could hear the staccato reports from the open exhaust of the motorcycle diminishing rapidly in the distance, indicating the speed of the pursued and the pursuer.

And then from the distance came a shot and then another and another. She leaned forward and spoke to her own driver. "Go on to Elmhurst," she said, "and then come back to the city on the St. Charles Road."

It was after two o'clock in the morning when the Lizard entered an apartment on Ashland Avenue which he had for several years used as a hiding-place when the police were hot upon his trail. The people from whom he rented the room were eminently respectable Jews who thought their occasional roomer what he represented himself to be, a special agent for one of the federal departments, a vocation which naturally explained the Lizard's long absences and unusual hours.

Once within his room the Lizard sank into a chair and wiped the perspiration from his forehead, although it was by no means a warm night. He drew a folded paper from his inside pocket, which, when opened, revealed a small piece of wrapping paper within. They were Murray's letter to Bince and the enclosure.

"Believe me," muttered the Lizard, "that was the toughest job I ever pulled off and all I gets is two pieces of paper, but I don't know but what they're worth it."

He sat for a long time looking at the papers in his hand, but he did not see them. He was thinking of other things: of prison walls that he had eluded so far through years of crime; of O'Donnell, whom he knew to be working on the Compton case and whose boast it had been that sooner or later he would get the Lizard; of what might naturally be expected were the papers in his hands to fall into the possession of Torrance's attorney. It would mean that Murray would be immediately placed in jeopardy, and the Lizard knew Murray well enough to know that he would sacrifice his best friend to save himself, and the Lizard was by no means Murray's best friend.

He realized that he knew more about the Compton murder case than any one else. He was of the opinion that he could clear it up if he were almost any one other than the Lizard, but with the record of his past life against him, would any one believe him? In order to prove his assertion it would be necessary to make admissions that might incriminate himself, and there would be Murray and the Compton millions against him; and as he pondered these things there ran always through his mind the words of the girl, "You and I are the only friends he has."

"Hell," ejaculated the Lizard as he rose from his chair and prepared for bed.

27

THE TRIAL

EDITH HUDSON spent a restless night, and early in the morning, as early as she thought she could reach him, she called the office of Jimmy's attorney. She told the lawyer that some new evidence was to have been brought in to him and asked if he had received it. Receiving a negative reply she asked that she be called the moment it was brought in.

All that day and the next she waited, scarcely leaving her room for fear that the call might come while she was away. The days ran into weeks and still there was no word from the Lizard.

Jimmy was brought to trial, and she saw him daily in the court-room and as often as they would let her she would visit him in jail. On several occasions she met Harriet Holden, also visiting him, and she saw that the other young woman was as constant an attendant at court as she.

The State had established as unassailable a case as might be built on circumstantial evidence.

Krovac had testified that Torrance had made threats against Compton in his presence, and there was no way in which Jimmy's attorneys could refute the perjured statement. Jimmy himself had come to realize that his attorney was fighting now for his life, that the verdict of the jury was already a foregone conclusion and that the only thing left to fight for now was the question of the penalty.

Daily he saw in the court-room the faces of the three girls who had entered so strangely into his life. He noticed, with not a little sorrow and regret, that Elizabeth Compton and Harriet Holden always sat apart and that they no longer spoke. He saw the effect of the strain of the long trial on Edith Hudson. She looked wan and worried, and then finally she was not in court one day, and later, through Harriet Holden, he learned that she was confined to her room with a bad cold.

Jimmy's sentiments toward the three women whose interests brought them daily to the court-room had undergone considerable change. The girl that he had put upon a pedestal to worship from afar, the girl to whom he had given an idealistic love, he saw now in another light. His reverence for her had died hard, but in the face of her arrogance, her vindictiveness and her petty snobbery it had finally succumbed, so that when he compared her with the girl who had been of the street the latter suffered in no way by the comparison.

Harriet Holden's friendship and loyalty were a never-ending source of wonderment to him, but he accepted her own explanation, which, indeed, was fair enough; that her innate sense of justice had compelled her to give him her sympathy and assistance.

Just how far that assistance had gone Jimmy did not know, though of late he had come to suspect that his attorney was being retained by Harriet Holden's father.

Bince appeared in the court-room only when necessity compelled his presence on the witness stand. The nature of the man's testimony was such that, like Krovac's, it was difficult of impeachment, although Jimmy was positive that Bince perjured himself, especially in a statement that he made of a conversation he had had with Mr. Compton the morning of the murder, in which he swore that Compton stated that he intended to discharge Torrance that day.

The effect of the trial seemed to have made greater inroads upon Bince than upon Jimmy. The latter gave no indication of nervous depression or of worry, while Bince, on the other hand, was thin, pale and haggard. His hands and face continually moved and twitched as he sat in the court-room or on the witness chair. Never for an instant was he at rest.

Elizabeth Compton had noticed this fact, too, and commented upon it one evening when Bince was at her home.

"What's the matter with you, Harold?" she asked. "You look as though you are on the verge of nervous prostration."

"I've had enough to make any man nervous," retorted Bince irritably. "I can't get over this terrible affair, and in addition I have had all the weight and responsibility of the business on my shoulders since, and the straightening out of your father's estate, which, by the way, was in pretty bad shape.

"I wish, Elizabeth," he went on, "that we might be married immediately. I have asked you so many times before, however, and you have always refused, that I suppose it is useless now. I believe that I would get over this nervous condition if you and I were settled down here together. I have no real home, as you know—the club is just a stopping place. I might as well be living at a hotel. If after the day's work I could come home to a regular home it would do me a world of good, I know. We could be married quietly. There is every reason why we should, especially now that you are left all alone."

"Just what do you mean by immediately?" she asked.

"To-morrow," he replied.

For a long time she demurred, but finally she acceded to his wishes, for an early marriage, though she would not listen to the ceremony being performed the following day. They reached a compromise on Friday morning, a delay of only a few days, and Harold Bince breathed more freely thereafter than he had for a long time before.

Mr. and Mrs. Harold Bince entered the courtroom late on Friday morning following the brief ceremony that had made them man and wife. It had been generally supposed that to-day the case would go to the jury as the evidence was all in, and the final arguments of the attorneys, which had started the preceding day, would be concluded during the morning session. It had been conceded that the judge's charge would be brief and perfunctory and there was even hope that the jury might return a verdict before the close of the afternoon session, but when Bince and his bride entered the courtroom they found Torrance's attorney making a motion for the admission of new evidence on the strength of the recent discovery of witnesses, the evidence of whom he claimed would materially alter the aspect of the case.

An hour was consumed in argument before the judge finally granted the motion. The first of the new witnesses called was an employee of the International Machine Company. After the usual preliminary questions the attorney for the defense asked him if he was employed in the plant on the afternoon of March 24. The reply was in the affirmative.

"Will you tell the jury, please, of any occurrence that you witnessed there that afternoon out of the ordinary?"

"I was working at my machine," said the witness, "when Pete Krovac comes to me and asks me to hide behind a big drill-press and watch what the assistant general manager done when he comes through the shop again. So I hides there and I saw this man Bince come along and drop an envelope beside Krovac's machine, and after he left I comes out as Krovac picks it up, and I seen him take some money out of it."

"How much money?" asked the attorney.

"There was fifty dollars there. He counted it in front of me."

"Did he say what it was for?"

"Yes, he said Bince gave it to him to croak this fellow"—nodding toward Jimmy.

"What fellow?" asked the attorney. "You mean Mr. Torrance, the defendant?"

"Yes, sir."

"And what else? What happened after that?"

"Krovac said he'd split it with me if I'd go along and help him."

"Did you?"

"Yes."

"What happened?"

"The guy beat up Krovac and come near croaking me, and got away."

"That is all," said the attorney.

The prosecuting attorney, whose repeated objections to the testimony of the witness had been overruled, waived cross-examination.

Turning to the clerk, "Please call Stephen Murray," said Jimmy's attorney.

Murray, burly and swaggering, took the witness chair. The attorney handed him a letter. It was the letter that Murray had written Bince enclosing the supposed I. W. W. threat.

"Did you ever see that before?" he asked.

Murray took the letter and read it over several times. He was trying to see in it anything which could possibly prove damaging to him.

"Sure," he said at last in a blustering tone of voice. "I wrote it. But what of it?"

"And this enclosure?" asked the attorney. He handed Murray the slip of soiled wrapping paper with the threat lettered upon it. "This was received with your letter."

Murray hesitated before replying. "Oh," he said, "that ain't nothing. That was just a little joke."

"You were seen in Feinheimer's with Mr. Bince on March— Do you recall the object of this meeting?"

"Mr. Bince thought there was going to be a strike at his plant and he wanted me to fix it up for him," replied Murray.

"You know the defendant, James Torrance?"

"Yes."

"Didn't he knock you down once for insulting a girl?" Murray flushed, but was compelled to admit the truth of the allegation.

"You haven't got much use for him, have you?" continued the attorney.

"No, I haven't," replied Murray.

"You called the defendant on the telephone a half or three-quarters of an hour before the police discovered Mr. Compton's body, did you not?"

Murray started to deny that he had done so. Jimmy's attorney stopped him. "Just a moment, Mr. Murray," he said, "if you will stop a moment and give the matter careful thought I am sure you will recall that you telephoned Mr. Torrance at that time, and that you did it in the presence of a witness," and the attorney pointed toward the back of the court-room. Murray looked in the direction that the other indicated and again he paled and his hand trembled where it rested on the arm of his chair, for seated in the back of the court-room was the head-waiter from Feinheimer's. "Now do you recall?" asked the attorney.

Murray was silent for a moment. Suddenly he

half rose from his chair. "Yes, I remember it," he said. "They are all trying to double-cross me. I had nothing to do with killing Compton. That wasn't in the deal at all. Ask that man there; he will tell you that I had nothing to do with killing Compton. He hired me and he knows," and with shaking finger Murray pointed at Mr. Harold Bince where he sat with his wife beside the prosecuting attorney.

28

THE VERDICT

FOR a moment there was tense silence in the courtroom which was broken by the defense's perfunctory "Take the witness" to the prosecuting attorney, but again cross-examination was waived.

"Call the next witness, please," and a moment later the Lizard emerged from the witness-room.

"I wish you would tell the jury," said the counsel for defense after the witness had been sworn, "just what you told me in my office yesterday afternoon."

"Yes, sir," said the Lizard. "You see, it was like this: Murray there sent for me and tells me that he's got a job for me. He wants me to go and crack a safe at the International Machine Company's plant. He said there was a fellow on the inside helping him, that there wouldn't be any watchman there that night and that in the safe I was to crack was some books and papers that was to be destroyed, and on top of it was three or four thousand dollars in pay-roll money that I was to have as my pay for the job. Murray told me that the guy on the inside who wanted the job done had been working some kind of a pay-roll graft and he wanted the records destroyed, and he also wanted to get rid of the guy that was hep to what he had been doin'. All that I had to do with it was go and crack the safe and get the records, which I was to throw in the river, and keep the money for myself, but the frame-up on the other guy was to send him a phone message that would get him at the plant after I got through, and then notify the police so they could catch him there in the room with the cracked safe.

"I didn't know who they were framin' this job on. If I had I wouldn't have had nothin' to do with it.

"Well, I goes to the plant and finds a window in the basement open just as they tells me it will be, but when I gets on the first floor just before I go up-stairs, I heard some one walking around up-stairs. I hid in the hallway while he come down. He stopped at the front door and lighted a cigarette and then he went on out, and I went up-stairs to finish the job.

"When I gets in Compton's office where the safe is I flashes my light and the first thing I see is Compton's body on the floor beside his desk. That kind of stuff ain't in my line, so I beats it out without crackin' the safe. That's all I know about it until I sees the papers, and then for a while I was afraid to say anything because this guy O'Donnell has it in for me, and I know enough about police methods to know that they could frame up a good case of murder against me. But after a while Miss

Hudson finds me and puts it up to me straight that this guy Torrance hasn't got no friends except me and her.

"Of course she didn't know how much I knew, but I did, and it's been worryin' me ever since. I was waiting, though, hopin' that something would turn up so that he would be acquitted, but I been watchin' the papers close, and I seen yesterday that there wasn't much chance, so here I am."

"You say that a man came down from Mr. Compton's office just before you went up? What time was that?"

"It was about ten o'clock, about half an hour before the cops finds Torrance there."

"And then you went up-stairs and found Mr. Compton dead?"

"You say this man that came down-stairs stopped and lighted a cigarette before he left the building. Did you see his face?"

"Yes, I did."

"Would you recognize him if you saw him again?"

"Sure."

"Look around the court-room and see if you can find him here."

"Sure I can find him. I seen him when I first came in, but I can't see his face because he's hiding behind the prosecuting attorney."

All eyes were turned in the direction of the prosecuting attorney to see Bince leap suddenly to his feet and lean forward upon the desk before him, supported by a trembling arm as he shook his finger at the Lizard, and in high-pitched tones screamed, "It's a lie! It's a lie!"

For a moment longer he stood looking wildly about the room, and then with rapid strides he crossed it to an open window, and before any one could interfere he vaulted out, to fall four stories to the cement sidewalk below.

For several minutes pandemonium reigned in the court-room. Elizabeth Compton Bince swooned, and when she regained consciousness she found herself in the arms of Harriet Holden.

"Take me home, Harriet," she asked; "take me away from this place. Take me to your home. I do not want to go back to mine yet."

Half an hour later, in accordance with the judge's charge to the jury, a verdict of "Not guilty" was rendered in the case of the People of Illinois *versus* James Torrance, Jr. Mr. Holden and Jimmy's attorney were the first to congratulate him, and the former insisted that he come home with him to dinner.

"I am sorry," said Jimmy; "I should like to immensely, but there is some one I must see first. If I may I should like to come out later in the evening to thank you and Miss Holden."

Jimmy searched about the court-room until he found the Lizard. "I don't know how to thank you," he said.

"Don't then," said the Lizard. "Who you ought to thank is that little girl who is sick in bed up on the north side."

"That's just where I am going now," said Jimmy. "Is she very sick?"

"Pneumonia," said the Lizard. "I telephoned

her doctor just before I came over here, and I guess if you want to see her at all you'd better hurry."

"It's not that bad, is it?" Jimmy said.

"I'm afraid it is," said the Lizard.

Jimmy lost no time in reaching the street and calling a taxi. A nurse admitted him to the apartment. "How is she?" he asked.

The nurse shook her head.

"Can she see any one?"

"It won't make any difference now," said the nurse, and Jimmy was led into the room where the girl, wasted by fever and suffering, lay in a half-comatose condition upon her narrow bed. Jimmy crossed the room and laid his hand upon her forehead, and at the touch she opened her eyes and looked up at him. He saw that she recognized him and was trying to say something, and he kneeled beside the bed so that his ear might be closer to her lips.

"Jimmy," she whispered, "you are free? Tell me."

He told her briefly of what had happened.

"I am so happy," she murmured. "Oh, Jimmy, I am so happy!"

He took one of her wasted hands in his own and carried it to his lips. "Not on the hand," she said faintly. "Just once, Jimmy, on the lips, before I die."

He gathered her in his arms and lifted her face to his. "Dear little girl," he said, "you are not going to die. It is not as bad as that."

She did not reply, but only clung to him tightly, and against his cheek he felt her tears and a little choking sob before she relaxed, and he laid her back again on her pillow. He thought she was dead then and he called the nurse, but she still breathed, though her eyes were closed. Jimmy sat down on the edge of the bed beside her and stroked her hand. After a while she roused again and opened her eyes.

"Jimmy," she said, "will you stay with me until I go?" The man could make no articulate response, but he pressed her hand reassuringly. She was silent again for some time. Once more she whispered faintly, so faintly that he had to lean close to catch her words:

"Miss Holden," she whispered, "she is a—good girl. It is—she—who hired—the attorney for you. Go to her—Jimmy—when I—am gone—she loves —you." Again there was a long pause. "Good-by —Jimmy," she whispered at last.

The nurse was standing at the foot of the bed. She came and put her hand on Jimmy's shoulder. "It is too bad," she said; "she was such a good girl."

"Yes," said Jimmy, "I think she was the best little girl I ever knew."

It was after nine o'clock when Jimmy, depressed and sorrowing, arrived at the Holden home. The houseman who admitted him told him that Mr. Holden had been called out, but that Miss Holden was expecting him, and he ushered Jimmy to the big living-room, and to his consternation he saw that Elizabeth Compton was there with Harriet. The latter came forward to greet him, and to his surprise the other girl followed her.

"I discovered to-day, Mr. Torrance," she said, "that I have wronged you. However unintentionally it was the fact remains that I might have done you a very great harm and injustice. I realize now how very different things might have been if I had listened to you and believed in you at first. Harriet told me that you were coming to-night and I asked to see you for just a moment to tell you this and also to ask you if you would continue with the International Machine Company.

"There is no one now whom I feel I would have so much confidence in as you. I wish you would come back and take charge for me. If you will tell me that you will consider it we will arrange the details later."

If an archangel had suddenly condescended to honor him with an invitation to assist in the management of Heaven Jimmy could not have been more surprised. He realized at what cost of pride and self-esteem the offer must have been made and acknowledgment of error. He told her that he would be very glad to assist her for the present, at least, and then she excused herself on the plea of nervous exhaustion and went to her room.

"Do you know," said Harriet, after Elizabeth had gone, "she really feels worse over her past attitude toward you than she does over Harold's death? I think she realizes now what I have told her from the first, that she never really loved him. Of course, her pride has suffered terribly, but she will get over that quickly enough.

"But do you know I have not had an opportunity before to congratulate you? I wish that I might have been there to have heard the verdict, but really you don't look half as happy as I should think you would feel."

"I am happy about that," said Jimmy, "but on top of my happiness came a sorrow. I just came from Edith's apartment. She died while I was there."

Harriet gave a little cry of shocked surprise. "Oh, Jimmy," she cried, laying her hand upon his arm. "Oh, Jimmy, I am so sorry!" It was the first time that she had ever addressed him by his given name, but there seemed nothing strange or unusual in the occurrence.

"She was such a good little girl," said Harriet.

It was strange that so many should use these same words in connection with Edith Hudson, and even this girl, so far removed from the sphere in which Little Eva had existed and who knew something of her past, could yet call her "good."

It gave Jimmy a new insight into the sweetness and charity of Harriet Holden's character. "Yes," he said, "her soul and her heart were good and pure."

"She believed so in you," said the girl. "She thought you were the best man who ever lived. She told me that you were the only really good man she had ever known, and her confidence and belief in you were contagious. You will probably never know all that she did for you. It was really she that imbued my father and his attorney with a belief in your innocence, and it was she who influenced the Lizard to take the stand in your behalf. Yes, she was a very good friend."

"And you have been a good friend," said Jimmy. "In the face of the same circumstances that turned Miss Compton against me you believed in me. Your generosity made it possible for me to be defended by the best attorney in Chicago, but more than all that to me has been your friendship and the consciousness of your sympathy at a time when, above all things, I needed sympathy. And now, after all you have done for me I came to ask still more of you."

"What do you want?" she asked.

She was standing very close to him, looking up in his face.

"You, Harriet," he said.

She smiled tremulously. "I have been yours for a long time, Jimmy, but you didn't know it."

(The end.)

CHARTER BOOKS—The best in mystery and suspense!

JOHN CREASEY

"Consistently the most satisfying of mystery novelists."
—The New York Post

☐ **A SPLINTER OF GLASS** 77800-3 $1.50
A tiny clue was all Superintendent West had to solve a huge gold theft—and a murder.

☐ **THEFT OF MAGNA CARTA** 80554-X $1.50
Scotland Yard searches for international thieves before a priceless treasure vanishes.

CHARTER BOOKS—The best in guides for healthier living!

☐ **INSTANT HEALTH THE NATURE WAY** 37079-9 $1.50
Put natural foods to work to fortify your body against disease. **Carlson Wade**

☐ **HERBAL REMEDIES** 32761-3 $1.95
The classic book of herbal medications, with centuries-old, proven remedies you can make. **Simmonite/Culpeper**

☐ **INFANT CARE** 37058-6 $1.95
by U.S. Dept. of Health, Education and Welfare.
The most famous book in America on pregnancy and child care, revised and updated.

- -

CHARTER BOOKS, Book Mailing Service
P.O. Box 690, Rockville Centre, N.Y. 11570

Please send me the titles checked above.

I enclose $ ______ . Add 50¢ handling fee per book.

Name ________________________________

Address ______________________________

City ______________ State ________ Zip ________

Cb

NICK CARTER

"Nick Carter out-Bonds James Bond."
—Buffalo Evening News

Exciting, international espionage adventure with Nick Carter, Killmaster N3 of AXE, the super-secret agency!

☐ THE ULTIMATE CODE 84308-5 $1.50
Nick Carter delivers a decoding machine to Athens—and finds himself in a CIA trap.

☐ BEIRUT INCIDENT 05378-5 $1.50
Killmaster infiltrates the Mafia to stop a new breed of underworld killer.

☐ THE NIGHT OF THE AVENGER 57496-3 $1.50
From Calcutta, to Peking, to Moscow, to Washington, AXE must prevent total war.

☐ THE SIGN OF THE COBRA 76346-4 $1.50
A bizarre religious cult plus a terrifying discovery join forces against N3.

☐ THE GREEN WOLF CONNECTION 30328-5 $1.50
Middle-eastern oil is the name of the game, and the sheiks were masters of terror.

Available wherever paperbacks are sold or use this coupon.

CHARTER BOOKS, Book Mailing Service
P.O. Box 690, Rockville Centre, N.Y. 11570

Please send me the titles checked above.

I enclose $ ________. Add 50¢ handling fee per book.

Name ________________

Address ________________

City ________ State ________ Zip ________

Db

NICK CARTER

"America's #1 espionage agent."
—Variety

Don't miss a single high-tension novel in the Nick Carter Killmaster series!

☐ THE JERUSALEM FILE 38951-5 $1.50
Nick battles Arab terrorists who have kidnapped the world's ten wealthiest men.

☐ THE FILTHY FIVE 23765-7 $1.50
Killmaster uncovers a Chinese plot to assassinate the President of the United States.

☐ SIX BLOODY SUMMER DAYS 76838-5 $1.50
The search for a stolen nuclear missile sends AXE into a desert death trap.

☐ THE KATMANDU CONTRACT 43200-X $1.50
The fate of Asia depended on a billion dollars in diamonds at the roof of the world.

☐ THE Z DOCUMENT 95485-5 $1.50
A power-hungry general in the Ethiopian Sahara stops at nothing to dominate the globe.

Available wherever paperbacks are sold or use this coupon.

CHARTER BOOKS, Book Mailing Service
P.O. Box 690, Rockville Centre, N.Y. 11570

Please send me the titles checked above.

I enclose $. Add 50¢ handling fee per book.

Name ____________________

Address ____________________

City ____________ State ______ Zip ______

Eb

CHARTER BOOKS

—the best in mystery and suspense!

JOHN DICKSON CARR

"...one of the all-time masters."
—Chicago Daily News

☐ BELOW SUSPICION 05394-7 $1.50
Dr. Gideon Fell plunges into a terrifying case of mass murder—and the devil.

☐ FIRE, BURN! 22910-7 $1.50
Inspector Cheviot hails a taxi on a foggy London night, and climbs out in 1829!

☐ THE PROBLEM OF THE GREEN CAPSULE 68052-6 $1.50
Master Detective Gideon Fell meets a fascinating man with a very dangerous hobby: poison.

Available wherever paperbacks are sold or use this coupon.

CHARTER BOOKS, Book Mailing Service
P.O. Box 690, Rockville Centre, N.Y. 11570

Please send me the titles checked above.

I enclose $ ______ . Add 50¢ handling fee per book.

Name ______________________

Address ______________________

City ______________ State ________ Zip ________

Fb

CHARTER BOOKS

—the best in mystery and suspense!

VICTOR CANNING

"One of the world's six best thriller writers."
—Reader's Digest

☐ **THE MASK OF MEMORY 52055-3 $1.75**
A chilling tale of espionage and counterespionage in a world without rules.

☐ **A FOREST OF EYES 22949-2 $1.75**
A British scientist working behind the iron curtain is dragged into a violent nightmare.

☐ **FIRECREST 22916-6 $1.75**
A dead scientist, his depraved mistress, a revenge-filled agent—and a terrifying secret.

Available wherever paperbacks are sold or use this coupon.

- -

CHARTER BOOKS, Book Mailing Service
P.O. Box 690, Rockville Centre, N.Y. 11570

Please send me the titles checked above.

I enclose $. Add 50¢ handling fee per book.

Name______________________________

Address ______________________________

City________________ **State** ______ **Zip**________

Gb